Seasoned Veteran

Roz Lee

MUSTANGS BASEBALL SERIES

CHAPTER ONE

Present Day - One week before Thanksgiving

Jake paused with his hand on the doorknob. Listening, he tried to pick out her voice, but the wooden blinds shading the glass-walled conference room muted the conversation inside. His heartbeat rivaled the stomping feet of the Mustangs' Thundering Herd rally—threatening to stampede right out of his chest.

Calm down. What's the worst she can do? No. Don't go there. That way be dragons. Think positive thoughts.

She's going to be happy to see you.

He forced to mind an image of Siobhan Flannery smiling up at him, her long, sable hair spread across his pillow, her features soft from her orgasm. It was an old image from weeks ago.

Before he'd fucked up. *Before* he'd walked away. *Before* he'd broken her heart. He hadn't stuck around to confirm the broken heart, but it hadn't been necessary. The pain had clouded her eyes when he callously ended their relationship the night the Mustangs lost their final playoff game.

She had every reason to hate him. Hell, he hated himself for what he'd done. It hadn't taken him long to figure out how big a mistake he'd made, but once he'd come to his senses, it had taken weeks to get back in her life in a way she couldn't ignore. Thank God, she'd decided to stay in Dallas through the holidays. If she'd gone home to D.C., he would have been on his own in figuring out how to get her attention.

He owed Bentley Randolph and his fiancée big time for setting today up for him. They'd both made their excuses to

2

the planning committee for the Crystal Ball, an annual costume event, softening the last minute blow by naming two good friends as their replacements. He'd never organized anything bigger than a poker night with his buddies, but he was willing to learn. He'd do anything for a second chance with Siobhan, even if it meant putting on Dallas' biggest charity event of the year all by himself.

A round of laughter inside the conference room reminded him he wasn't going to have to do this alone. According to Ashley, most of the work had already been done. All he needed to do was follow up on the things Bentley had been responsible for, most of which she'd actually taken care of herself Which meant Siobhan had inherited a double dose of problems.

Time to man up. Face the music. Beg. Grovel. All of the above.

Taking a cleansing breath then letting it out, he turned the knob.

Siobhan laughed along with the others seated around the large, oval conference table, though it almost hurt to do so. She couldn't remember the last time she'd thought something was humorous.

Yes, you do.

Before.

When you were alive.

Technically, she was alive, but to say she was living wouldn't be accurate. *Existing.* Her body functioned on a basic level. She breathed, she ate—though she'd lost weight—she slept, often taking long naps in the afternoon when fatigue weighed heavy on her shoulders. Life had lost its sparkle.

Before, she'd seen the potential for happiness in everyone. She'd firmly believed there was a special someone out there for everybody. She'd believed in happily ever after. She'd made her living on happily ever afters.

Looking at the smiling faces ringing the table, she forced her lips to curve upward. They were a nice enough bunch, she supposed. They'd put months of work into the charity event taking place in a few weeks only to be saddled with her, a last minute stand-in for Ashley. The other woman had found herself in over her head, trying to keep up with her responsibility to the committee while planning her own wedding for the week after Christmas.

Add the stress of bringing on Siobhan's brother, Sean, as the new anchor for one of the syndicated television sports-talk shows Ashley was in charge of, and the woman had hit the proverbial brick wall.

Enter Siobhan, a broken woman who hadn't been out in public in weeks, who admittedly had nothing to do since she'd mostly given up on her career as a romance novelist. Not writing a single word since her break-up with Jake didn't constitute a forfeit of her career, but it didn't bode well either.

Ever since Jake ended their *affair*—she refused to call it a relationship because the term indicated a level of commitment their time together had never reached at least on Jake's part—the only story ideas that came to mind had a decidedly dark tint to them. None had a happy ending, which, of course, was the definition of a romance novel.

In truth, she should be grateful to

Ashley for dropping the Crystal Ball committee in her lap. Hiding out from the world, watching taped reruns of reality TV shows about dysfunctional families in order to make her own situation seem better by comparison, hadn't been working for her. No matter how pathetic the on-screen families appeared, she knew in her heart, her story was worse. Everyone had warned her about the Mustangs' batting coach, but she'd been too dazzled by him to see what they were saying was true. She'd believed from the very beginning of their association she was the exception. He wouldn't leave *her* when the season was over. He loved her, he just wasn't ready to admit it yet.

When, the Mustangs' season ended on a loss to the Claim Jumpers, Jake told her it was over before the stadium lights had gone out.

She sighed, letting her gaze fall on the thick binder on the table in front of her. Between the shiny blue covers lurked details on everything Ashley had been in charge of. Siobhan had looked the contents over before coming, finding it mostly in order. All she needed to do was follow up with the vendors Ashley had talked to, make sure everything was on track for the early December event, then she would be done.

The job was easy enough. It was the other part that bothered her. She'd have to go out in public and face each day with a purpose—something she hadn't done since that fateful night.

The meeting should have commenced a few minutes ago, but even though no one had mentioned it, she'd gotten the impression they were waiting on someone else to arrive.

The door opened. The chairperson, Mr. Whitaker, stood as did the hair on the back of her neck.

"There he is," he said.

She didn't need him to say more. Every cell in her body tingled with awareness. Keeping her head down, she snuck a peek through her eyelashes at his long legs encased in expensive trousers held up with a thin leather belt around a trim waist.

Murmurs went around the table regarding the impeccably dressed newcomer. She swallowed hard, willing the floor to open up like in some James Bond movie. Dropping into a tank of hungry sharks sounded better than staying where she was. Anywhere was better than being in the same room with Jake Tulleson.

Cursing her insane need to feast on the perfection of his body, she allowed her gaze to creep higher until it reached his face. He was looking straight at her! Their gazes locked.

What is he doing here? Is he looking for me?

Her stupid heart tripped all over itself as the fantasy took root. A clip from one of her favorite old movies flashed across her brain—Richard Gere in a white officer's uniform striding purposely across the factory floor, intent on sweeping his true love off to her happily ever after. Siobhan almost came out of her chair, ready to fling herself into Jake's arms, before common sense overruled. He wasn't the dashing, romantic hero. This was real life. The bastard who'd just arrived had made it perfectly clear the last time she saw him that he didn't do happily ever after, at least not the shared kind.

Her heart took a swan dive straight to her toes where it flopped around like a fish on dry land.

She blinked, breaking the invisible connection between them. Jake turned his attention to Mr. Whitaker who was babbling about their other new committee member.

"Ladies. Gentlemen," Mr. Whitaker said. "Allow me to introduce Jake Tulleson, who after an illustrious career behind home plate for the Jetsetters, took to coaching. For the last five years, he's been the batting coach for the Mustangs."

The two men shook hands. "Welcome, Jake. We understand why Bentley had to relinquish his duties. He has a lot on his plate with his upcoming nuptials." The comical face he put on for the gathering was received with a hearty round of laughter. He turned back to the new recruit. "How could we be put out when he sent us such a splendid replacement?"

"Thanks, Mr. Whitaker." Jake scanned the assembled group. "I'm happy to be here. Bentley filled me in on the tasks assigned to him. I'm confident I can see them to completion—with your help, of course."

The committee leader motioned with his hand. "If you'll have a seat, we'll get this meeting underway, so we can all go on about our business."

It was like being in a 3-D horror movie. She was trapped in her seat by the creature advancing on her—only this monster was real, shaking hands, smiling and greeting every single committee member as he made his way to the one empty spot at the table. The one next to her.

Jake pulled the chair out. His fingers gripped the edge of the table to pull himself forward. Her gaze landed on his hands, hands that knew her body better than any others on earth, including her own

"Jake," Mr. Whitaker said. "Bentley mentioned you and Ms. Flannery are acquainted, which will surely make your tasks easier, as your predecessors were working together on a number of projects."

She was going to kill Ashley for

leaving out that crucial bit of information. This entire thing smelled of a setup.

"Yes." He turned to her. "We're well acquainted." He had the audacity to smile at her as if he hadn't stomped all over her heart a few weeks ago. "It's good to see you again."

She nodded. "Jake."

Folding her trembling hands in her lap, she focused on the two-inch thick binder Ashley had passed on to her compared to the non-existent one Jake had brought. If her heart could have sunk any further, it would have, but it still flopped around at her feet, no doubt gasping its last breath as reality dawned.

Like the too-stupid-to-live character in the horror movie, she remained in her seat and allowed Jake to drop his net over her. "Don't worry about us. We'll work together just fine," he told the group. "We're going to be stuck together like glue until this thing is over, to make sure nothing is left undone."

She didn't hear much after Jake's declaration. The meeting continued on around her. When it came to things she, and apparently Jake, were in charge of, he charmed them with promises to get up to speed quickly, saying they would report back at the meeting next week, if that was all right with the committee.

Just like that, she was snared in his net. He'd obviously gone to the trouble of setting this up, because she sure as hell hadn't done it. But for the life of her, she couldn't imagine why.

At the close of the meeting, Siobhan stayed in her seat while Jake stood to shake hands with every committee member as they filed out. Closing the door behind the last one, he remained there, his back pressed to the wood, his hands stuck in the pockets of his dress slacks. He looked like a model in an advertisement for erectile dysfunction medication—too young to need the product but old enough men who did need it would see him and think, "Product X will make me look like him, then I'll get any woman I want!"

Her heart still lay on the floor, too weak to resist if he chose to stomp on it again.

"You look beautiful today."

"Shut up, Jake! You don't have any

right to say things like that to me anymore." As she got to her feet, she clutched her new binder to her breasts as if it were armor. "Not after the way you ended things."

"I'm sorry. I know I was an ass, but I've come to my senses. I love you."

Oh no. No. No. No. She shook her head. "No you don't. If you did, you wouldn't have left."

"I think I fell in love with you the night we met. I know I felt something when I sank my cock in your hot pussy. I remember because the feeling scared the living daylights out of me. I spent the rest of the time we were together telling myself you were just another good fu...."

A red haze glazed over her eyes. She understood how a person could commit murder. If she had anything sharper than a ballpoint pen, she'd be tempted to skewer him with it. She tightened her grasp on her notebook, flattening her breasts with it until she felt the physical pain. That was so much easier to deal with than the ache in her heart. She tapped her toe, unable to squelch her anger entirely. "Go ahead. Finish what you were going to say. Don't leave me hanging. I was just another good…what?"

He pulled his hands from his pockets, fisting them on his hips as he straightened away from the door. "Fuck, Siobhan! I told myself you were just another good fuck. I knew it wasn't the truth, but I wasn't ready to admit you meant more to me."

"You son-of-a-bitch." She advanced on him. Whatever love she'd harbored for him since he'd cut her out of his life shattered the minute he confessed to using her for months. "I don't know what hole you crawled into when you left here last month, but you can go back to it. I loved you, Jake, but I was nothing more than a good fuck to you. Well, go fuck yourself."

With as much dignity as she could muster, she stormed past him into the corridor. Spying the stairwell door at the end of the hall, she stumbled in that direction, managing to descend a couple of flights before her legs gave out. Squeezing her eyes shut, she willed herself not to cry.

Never again. He's not worth it.

She'd already spent too many hours dehydrating herself over Jake Tulleson. "Go to hell, you bastard." Fumbling in her purse, she found a tissue to dab at the corners of her eyes. She blew her nose into the thin, soggy square. "You told him."

Her voice echoed off the bare concrete walls, making her sound bolder than she actually was. "Why did you come back to torment me?" she asked the ringing silence. "Wasn't breaking me in half once enough for you?"

She sniffled. She didn't care what Ashley had to do between now and her wedding, Siobhan was going to dump the big-assed binder back in her lap then get the hell out of Dodge. Dallas. Whatever. Her friend had meant well, she was sure of it, but no way was she spending another minute in Jake's company, much less be glued to his side for the three weeks until the Crystal Ball.

No. Fucking. Way.

Her vocabulary had slipped a notch or two, she noted.

"Fuck you, Jake."

It felt good to say what she felt

without censoring herself.

She tried the words out again, louder. As the echo faded, it seemed to take some of the tension in her body with it. After repeating the phrase several more times, she began to feel more in control. Gathering her things, she descended to the bottom floor.

The stairwell opened to an inside lobby. To her right was a glass door leading to the parking lot where she'd left her car.

Perfect.

She climbed into the older, secondhand sedan she'd recently purchased so she wouldn't be dependent on her brother, Ashley, or Bentley for transportation. If only she'd made the decision to buy a car sooner. Perhaps she never would have met Jake....

CHAPTER TWO

Two months earlier.

September 12th

Siobhan pressed the accelerator hard, speeding across the parking lot to the player entrance. The Mustangs' game had been over for nearly an hour, which meant she was close to two hours late. Screeching to a stop in front of the two men conversing beneath a weak security lamp, she slammed the gearshift on the late-model SUV into Park then pushed her door open at the same time.

"I'm so sorry!" She climbed out of the driver's seat. "I should have realized the traffic would be insane once the game was over. You should have seen the parking guy." She rolled her eyes. "You would have thought I was trying to break you out of prison or something."

Bentley Randolph, the car's owner and her temporary landlord, laughed. "No problem. I had a few things to discuss with Jake."

Relieved she wasn't in hot water for her tardiness, she shifted her gaze to Bentley's companion. He stood mostly in shadow, but she easily catalogued all the important things. He was tall, lean, and he knew how to dress—dark suit, white shirt. She guessed his tie picked up the color of his suit or possibly the hue of his eyes in its geometric pattern. Her overactive writer's imagination filled in the missing details just as she would for one of her characters.

"Oh, did I interrupt?"

Jake-the-mystery-man stepped into

the light, a set of car keys jiggling in one hand. "No. I was just waiting to make sure Bent had a ride before I left. Can't have one of our star players hitchhiking home after a game." His deep voice vibrated through her like the bass line of her favorite song. She shivered in the warm night air. *Oh, yum.*

His tone indicated he wasn't in the least put out by the wait. He turned to Bentley. "Please tell me this isn't your fiancée."

"No," Bentley laughed. "This is Sean Flannery's sister, Siobhan. She's staying with me so she can be close enough to help her brother. She's been using Sean's car, but he's driving himself around again. I let her borrow mine today on the condition she didn't leave me sitting here without a ride home. Siobhan, this is Jake Tulleson, the Mustangs' batting coach."

"Nice to meet you, Mr. Tulleson." She addressed her benefactor. "I'm really sorry, Bentley. I lost all track of time. I found some really interesting articles, though." After her brother broke his hip falling into the dugout in pursuit of a fly ball, Bentley offered Sean the use of his

19

pool house while he went through his physical therapy. Since the pool house only had one bedroom, he'd opened his house to her so she could remain close by to help. He and his fiancée had been incredibly generous—all the more reason her screw up tonight weighed on her conscience. The last thing she wanted was for either of them to think she was ungrateful.

"What kind of research?" Jake asked, moving around the hood of the car. The headlights briefly illuminated him, giving her more details to fill in—tanned skin, a firm, cleanly shaved jaw, a nice haircut. He moved like an athlete, though she didn't remember hearing Sean speak of him. He paused near the front tire. His lips were full, his nose narrow. Thin lines fanned out from the corners of his eyes, giving him an air of maturity that piqued her interest. She'd about had her fill of boys masquerading as men.

"Um…I was looking up period dress for women in Texas during the Republic years, 1836-1846."

He was close enough she could see the flecks of gray at his temples. His eyes were blue. As she suspected earlier, there were dots of the same color in his tie. The tiny lines, like parenthesis, bracketing his mouth, captivated her. She'd always been a sucker for well-placed punctuation.

"Fascinating." His voice rumbled like distant thunder, vibrating through her all the way to her toes.

Siobhan had the oddest feeling he wasn't referring to the research she was doing for her next series of romance novels.

"I think so, too." She hoped he would hear in her words the same thing she'd heard in his. He was the most fascinating man she'd seen in...forever.

"Are you all done with your research?"

She shook her head. "No. I bought some books at the museum."

"I'd love to see your books."

The slight hesitation before he said that last word made her heart gallop. It must have run off with her good sense because she heard herself say, "I'd like to show you my books. When?"

"Now is good." He moved around the open car door.

21

Siobhan looked at his outstretched hand then ducked back into the car to grab her purse and the bag from the museum. When she straightened, his hand still waited for hers. She placed her palm over his. Tiny pinpricks of electricity skittered up her arm, across her shoulder then down to her breasts. Her nipples tingled, forming tight buds.

Someone cleared his throat. Siobhan looked around to find Bentley watching them.

"Oh! Bentley. You don't mind if I give you your car back right here, do you?"

He smiled. "Not at all. Jake will see you get home okay."

It wasn't a question, but a directive aimed at his batting coach.

"I'll see no harm comes to Flannery's little sister." Jake pulled her away from Bentley's SUV and toward the only other vehicle in the lot.

He opened the door for her, and she scooted into the expensive sports car. Even though it was well past sundown in mid-September, summer had yet to release its hold on North Texas. The interior was an oven. Adjusting her legs on the hot leather seat, Siobhan briefly wondered if she was being incredibly stupid to go off with a virtual stranger. When he opened the opposite door and folded himself into the driver's seat, all doubt vanished.

He cranked the car before adjusting the climate control system. Cool air rushed from the dashboard vents, raising gooseflesh on her arms. Beneath the thin cotton sundress she'd put on that morning, her nipples stood to attention.

They sat in silence until Bentley's SUV pulled out of the lot. Alone in the darkened car with a man she'd met less than five minutes earlier, she tried to find even a kernel of trepidation, but came up empty. Maybe it was the obvious age difference or the air of confidence surrounding him, but he made her feel safe—and horny. It had been a long time since she'd felt this kind of sexual attraction. Hell, she'd never experienced anything quite like this, as if she couldn't wait to get naked with a man. Inexplicably, she knew Jake was the kind of man who would take his time with a woman, even if he hadn't wasted a minute getting her into his car.

He remained silent until Bentley's taillights were nothing more than pinpoints of light in the distance. "You know I don't give a damn about the books in that bag."

His deep voice stroked every taut string in her body, making her shiver with need. It had been way too long since she'd had sex, and she'd never been with a guy who oozed sex appeal the way Jake did. He was a man of few words, but every one sounded like a promise to her starved hormones.

"I never thought you did." She dared to look at him. He was watching her. A thrill shot through her. In that super-charged instant, she was positive he saw more than what the sodium light over the player's gate and the backlit dashboard could reveal. She felt exposed—naked.

"The only game I play is baseball."

She took his statement for the warning it clearly was. "No games," she agreed, though she wasn't sure exactly what kind of games she could possibly play with this man.

"Take off your panties."

Her breath caught in her throat at the blatant order. The car idled beneath her like the giant cat it was named after, a sensual caress that made her hyperaware of her lady parts. It didn't help that they'd been throbbing ever since she first heard his voice purring in the darkness.

"No games, Siobhan. Take them off. Loop them over the mirror."

She lifted her purse and museum bag off her lap. He took them, depositing them somewhere behind her seat. Raising her hips, she reached under her skirt. It took some fancy shimmying in the tight confines to work her panties off, but eventually she pulled them free then hung them over the rearview mirror.

Long, masculine fingers hooked the crotch. "You're wet." She was grateful for the dark interior as her skin heated at his observation. "Recline your seat."

Wordlessly, she found the lever on the side of her seat. Lowering the backrest as far as it would go, she went down with it, watching his face all the way for any indication this little scene affected him even half as much as it affected her.

Jake Tulleson was as cool as a cucumber.

No problem. She wasn't looking for a relationship, just some sex—preferably good sex—while she was in Dallas helping her brother recover from his most recent hip injury. In a few months, she would head home with a treasure trove of memories she could use to spice up her writing. Never again would a reader complain the sex scenes in her books were dull. She had hoped to come up with a suitable research partner at some point, but not this soon, and she'd never dreamed she'd find someone as promising as Jake Tulleson.

"Hike up your skirt. I want to see you."

Grasping the fabric near her waist, she gathered her skirt up an inch at a time until her mound was exposed to his gaze. He didn't say anything for the longest, just looked.

"Beautiful." He reached across her, closed his hand over the seatbelt, fastening it for her.

He put the car in gear and drove out of the parking lot. Unable to see much from her position, she watched Jake drive.

The beast of an automobile purred, reacting to his commands as if it understood he was its master. He held the steering wheel and operated the gearshift with supreme confidence. Imagining him touching her in the same way, she tingled with anticipation, her body humming right along with the powerful engine propelling them through the night.

Suddenly, her inexperience compared to his sexual skill seemed like an insurmountable obstacle. He was used to full-grown cats—felines in need of taming. She was nothing more than a kitten with too much curiosity for her own good. She should tell him what this was all about before it went any further. It wasn't right to use him for the sake of a few book sales. Up until he'd stepped out of the shadows and illuminated her world a few minutes ago, she'd had a viable plan to fill in the blanks of her sexual experience. She just hadn't yet gotten up the nerve to watch any of the videos she'd located on the Internet.

The car careened around a sharp curve. Her panties swayed on their makeshift hanger.

I've got to tell him.

She tried to sit up, intent on telling Jake the truth about why she had accepted his invitation, but a big hand left the steering wheel to press her back down.

"Don't move."

"Jake." She smoothed her skirt down then made another attempt to sit upright. This time, he didn't stop her.

"What? Second thoughts?"

"Yes. No." She reached for her panties but he wrapped his hand around her wrist, stopping her.

"Leave them there." When she released her grip, he returned her hand to her lap. "We're almost home. Save what you have to say till we get there."

At least he's being reasonable. All she needed to do was explain the situation. Be up front with him. Then he'd take her back to Bentley's house. Maybe he'd even offer to answer a few questions for her, like how a man knew what a woman liked or how he knew where to touch a woman to make her forget why she shouldn't remove her panties and ride through the streets of Dallas with her skirt hiked to her waist.

Her face flamed. She looked out the passenger window in hopes he wouldn't notice. They'd entered an upscale neighborhood that looked suspiciously like Bentley's. "Where are we going?"

"I'm taking you home."

Heat warmed her skin again, but this time humiliation fueled the fire inside her. He didn't want her, after all. When had he recognized she wasn't his type? Had she been too eager to remove her panties or was it when she tried to take them back?

"I don't want to go home."

He pulled to the curb with the skill of a racecar driver squeezing into a pit stall then slammed the gearshift into Park.

"What the hell are you talking about? I thought we had an agreement."

"What?" She glanced at the street lined with private walled yards behind security gates. It looked familiar, but had she jumped to the wrong conclusion? "This is the way to Bentley's."

His shoulders relaxed. "I live a few blocks from here," he explained. "Do you want me to take you to Bent's? Or do you want to come home with me?"

She'd squelched good sense twice tonight. Once when she got in Jake's car, then again when she'd blurted out that she didn't want to go home. The voice of reason tried again. "We should talk."

"No talking. Either you want to have sex with me or you don't. Which is it?"

The big cat purred softly under the hood of the car. *Sex. That's all this is.* Jake was years older than her and probably centuries wiser when it came to sexual matters. That's what she needed. One night with him would give her enough material to write an entire series of books.

"Your house."

"Say it. Say you want me to fuck you."

She swallowed hard. A Dreamsicle-colored cat sauntered across the road just on the edge of the Jaguar's headlight beam. A cat out on the prowl. *That's me.* She looked at him. "I want you to fuck me."

CHAPTER THREE

Present - Thanksgiving

Day

Jake popped the frozen tray into the
microwave then leaned against the
counter to wait for his Thanksgiving
dinner to nuke. The Cowboys' game
played silently on the big-screen TV in the
den, visible through the arched kitchen
doorway.

He'd come back to Dallas with the intention of spending this holiday, and every other one in the future, with Siobhan. But he'd fucked up—again. What in heaven's name had possessed him to tell her she'd been nothing but a good fuck?

"Idiot." He cringed at the sound of his own voice. Other than a trip to the grocery store for essentials, he hadn't left his house since what was supposed to have been the day his life changed for the better. But instead of improving his lot, he'd sent it spiraling down the crapper.

"You really fucked it up this time."

The microwave dinged. Turning, he picked up the discarded box to read the instructions again. After stirring the crystallized meal then resetting the timer, he crossed the room to stare out the window overlooking the backyard. The grass was mostly brown with a few patches of mottled green. The gray sky reflecting off the black-bottomed pool mirrored his mood—gloomy and desolate.

He'd spent a month in Colorado, coming up with reasons he shouldn't or couldn't be with Siobhan. Near the top of the list was their age difference. In retrospect, the fifteen years between them had been the armor he'd used to keep her at a distance when they'd been together. It had also been the reason he'd ended their relationship.

Being truthful with himself, he had imagined introducing Siobhan to his daughter more than once, but each time he'd conjured up the scenario, he'd seen himself as some sort of pervert. So, he ran. Just like he'd done a dozen other times in the past with women he had no intention of bringing into his private life.

He chuckled. At the sound of the microwave buzzer, he turned to remove his solitary dinner from the oven. Sitting at the breakfast bar, all alone with his plastic tray of steaming holiday food, he paused to absorb the feeling. He'd been alone more times than he could count over the years. A professional baseball player's lifestyle wasn't conducive to relationships—he'd learned that early on. Over the years, he'd used that knowledge like a get-out-of-jail-free card, pulling it whenever a woman got too close.

Rearranging his sorry meal with his fork, he thought about where his stupidity had gotten him. He was alone by choice, lonely due to the fact he was an idiot.

"I thought of you as just another good fuck." Spearing a precisely formed piece of limp turkey, he shook his head. "I don't know what is more pathetic, this meal or you, Tulleson."

Chewing, he tried to focus on the football game flickering across the screen. An annual tradition on Thanksgiving, it usually held his attention no matter where he was. For the last twenty-something years, he'd watched the game with his family. Every other year, he'd brought his best girl with him to show off.

This year, he'd talked to his parents earlier in the day, assured them everything was fine, he'd be spending the day with friends. His daughter, Kelly had been full of questions he'd dodged with questions of his own. "What do you want for Christmas? What's this I hear about you wanting to study abroad next year?"

God, she was growing up so fast. No. Make that had grown up. His little girl was twenty, with two years of college behind her, but older and wiser than him by decades. She'd been the one to notice his mood, to probe him with inquiries until he told her the truth. He'd expected her to hate him for falling in love with a woman just five years older than her, but he'd underestimated his daughter, which was nothing new. She'd been outsmarting him since the day she was born—and he couldn't be prouder of that fact.

Her mother had done a fantastic job raising her, and he'd done a fantastic job of letting her. They'd been too young, too stupid, to get married, much less have a kid, so they'd compromised, passed on the marriage, but kept the kid. Before Kelly was born, he'd gone off to the Minor League. It wasn't long after that he'd been called up to the Majors. They'd worked out a deal where he had Kelly in the off-season, but that meant living nearby so his daughter wouldn't have to change schools or disrupt her routine any more than necessary. Rotating holidays with both their families developed naturally over the years.

He was a lucky man. Though he'd never loved his daughter's mother the way a man should love the mother of his child, the two of them had managed to work things out so she had the best both her parents could offer. She'd never wanted for anything financially, had received love and guidance from both their families. His heart warmed just thinking about the special person his daughter had grown to be.

It was because of her he'd returned to Dallas. Instead of thinking her father was a perv when he told her about Siobhan, she'd helped him pack his suitcase, admonishing him not to come back until he could bring the woman he loved with him.

Forcing another bite of processed turkey down his throat, he feared he'd never see the rest of his family again if he followed Kelly's instructions to the letter. For a few weeks, he'd had it all, he'd just been too stupid to see it.

CHAPTER FOUR

Two months earlier -

September 12th

Damn. He'd died a thousand deaths waiting for Siobhan to give him the green light to proceed. If she'd said no, he would have driven her home to Bentley's house, but for reasons he couldn't explain, he knew he would have hated doing it. Siobhan loved her brother enough to spend months caring for him. Given what he suspected about Sean Flannery's sexual orientation, her love was unconditional.

Another turn sent her panties swaying again. Cool air blowing from a center vent acted like a diffuser, carrying Siobhan's scent throughout the car, especially when he took a curve. Inhaling deeply, he committed her bouquet to memory. He couldn't wait to bury his face between her legs so he could taste her. She'd be as sweet as honey and as intoxicating as twenty-year-old whiskey.

Hell, she couldn't be much more than twenty years old, herself. Too young for him, but old enough to consent. He'd have her tonight then send her back to her babysitter. He smirked, remembering Bentley's admonishing tone. Sean might not know what his little sister was up to, but Bentley did, and he wasn't thrilled about it.

One night, Bent. That's all I want. I'll send your pet home well used, but unharmed. I promise.

"Are you old enough to drink," he asked, leading the way into the den where he kept a decently stocked bar.

"I'm twenty-five."

He nodded, popping the stopper on a bottle of scotch that was older than her. *Shit.* He poured two fingers into two glasses, handing her one. "I'm beginning to feel like a pervert."

She took a sip of the dark amber liquid, swallowed then smiled her appreciation for the libation. "This is good. I grew up on Jamison's."

He raised an eyebrow. "Grew up on it?"

"Rumor has it my grandfather on my dad's side put it in my baby bottle. I have my doubts about the truth of the story, but my mom claims she rubbed it on my gums when I was teething. Warning— don't cough in the Flannery household or you'll have a cup of tea, liberally spiked, in your hand before you know it."

"Sounds very practical to me."

"It's not exactly modern medicine, but it works." Her words died off. Maybe she realized how trivial the conversation was in light of why she was drinking whiskey in his den while he had her panties in his pocket. She sipped again—

for courage, perhaps—and asked, "How old are you?"

"Forty-one in a few months." *Ancient. Old enough to be her father. Too old for an angel like her.*

"You don't look it. I would have thought thirty-five, tops."

"Thanks, I think." He swirled the liquid in his glass, watching it rise and fall around the sides of the crystal tumbler. "Why are you here?"

She finished her drink in one last gulp. "I thought that was obvious. I'm attracted to you. I want to sleep with you."

He smiled. "Hon, there won't be much sleeping in my bed tonight." Not if he could help it, or stay awake for it. Getting old was a bitch.

She helped herself to his whiskey decanter, pouring three fingers into her glass. "You know what I meant. Are you trying to scare me away by being crude?"

"Hell, no," he said, meaning it. "I told you I don't play games. I needed to hear you say it, just so we both know what's going to happen. I don't want you leaving here in the morning thinking things went too far."

"As best as I can tell, they haven't gone anywhere, except you have my panties, and I'm in danger of getting soused on your liquor."

He set his unfinished drink on the nearest flat surface then crossed the room to stand toe-to-toe with her. She lifted her face. Their gazes met. Damn, she looked a lot younger than twenty-five, but she was of legal age for everything he had in mind. That was all that mattered.

"Let me see if I can get you intoxicated some other way." He was already half drunk on her scent, and he'd yet to do more than hold her hand and glance at her snatch. It wasn't fair such a little girl had that kind of effect on him. She made him feel old and young all at the same time, and he didn't have a clue what to do about it.

Her lips were plump, stung from the strong spirits. Without touching her anywhere else, he lowered his head, covering her mouth with his. Soft. Warm. Perfect. He tasted the whiskey on her tongue, but there was something underneath, something unique and more intoxicating. He angled his head to get a better fit then she did the same. They came together like animals mating. Sucking, biting, taking, giving, tasting and feasting. He'd kissed plenty of women since his adolescent days, but none of them had stolen his sanity the way this one did. It was one kiss!

He'd meant to seduce but found himself surrendering to the passion growing between them. She wasn't innocent, but he could tell she was learning as she went, taking everything he did, turning it back on him until he was no longer sure who was seducing whom. Sweet God, her mouth was made for kissing—and so much more.

Reluctantly breaking the kiss, he stepped back. He took the glass from her hand. Carrying the drink, he led her to the stairs with his free hand on her ass. God, he loved firm women. He couldn't wait to get her out of her dress. Her sundress looked like one of those no bra things—a marvel of modern technology if he'd ever seen one. One zipper then, if he was correct, she'd be naked.

She remained silent as he set her

drink on his nightstand then removed his clothes. He took good care of himself. Years of having to do so in order to play baseball had ingrained on his life. He worked out every morning as religiously as he showered and brushed his teeth. The gym wasn't a fountain of youth, but it kept him lean, his muscles hard. Tonight, the hardest part of him sprang free as he shoved his boxers to his ankles. His dick wasn't enormous, but he had plenty to offer. No one had ever complained and, from the look on Siobhan's face, she was suitably impressed. At her age, she couldn't have seen all that many, but still, her approval filled him with pride.

"Can I," she asked, reaching for him.

"It's all yours." He thought she only wanted to touch him, but when she sat on the edge of the bed, motioning him forward, he knew better. She spread her legs. He stepped between them. His cock bobbed against her lips, sending shock waves of pleasure up his spine. She wrapped one hand around the base— reached for her whiskey glass with the other. He watched helplessly as she turned her head, tilted the tumbler to her lips, and drank.

Her whiskey-soaked tongue swirled around the head of his dick, spreading liquid fire across the sensitive skin. He hissed at the jolt to his nervous system. It was all he could do to remain upright. Then she closed her lips over him, taking his cock in, one fiery inch at a time.

"Christ almighty!" He fisted his hands in her hair. Holding on for dear life, he prayed he wouldn't collapse. Her mouth was wicked, wet heat searing his flesh. Killing him. He was on fire inside and out. As she worked the length of his shaft, igniting flames then dowsing them with cool air over and over again, he clung to her for support. He should put a stop to it before she ruined him, but he couldn't. Even if his life depended on it, he couldn't.

His dick popped free. For a second he thanked God he'd survived, but she'd only paused to take another drink. Holding his cock high, she dipped her head. Her tongue swiped across his balls. He saw stars. Before he could stop her, she swallowed his dick again. Her wicked tongue swirled around his girth. Her cheeks hollowed, applying the most devastating suction he'd ever felt. It was like someone strapped a jet pack to his genitals then lit the fuse. He rocketed straight to the stratosphere.

He couldn't stop from coming. His hips jerked. His testicles were fireballs burning through his groin. Cum jetted from him in a hot stream that scalded his insides and fried every synapse in his brain.

Holy shit.

CHAPTER FIVE

Two months earlier -

September 12th

Siobhan dropped to the bed, her arms flung wide, Jake Tulleson on the floor between her legs. The back of his head rested against her aching pussy—a first for her. She could hear him breathing, so she knew he was alive. She'd read about the trick with the whiskey, somewhere, and had always wanted to try it, never believing it would produce such positive results.

She licked her lips. Running her tongue around the inside of her mouth, she savored every last trace of his orgasm. For the first time in her limited sexual experience, she felt powerful. She wanted to tell the whole world of her triumph. She, little Siobhan Flannery, had knocked the knees out from under a real man. Despite Jake's present state, he was all man—a seasoned veteran on the baseball field and in bed. Yet, he lay crumpled at her feet, panting as if he'd beat out a throw to third base for a stand-up triple.

"You okay?" She reached down to run her fingers through his hair. In better lighting, indoors, she noticed more than a touch of gray throughout, but not a bald spot in sight. Like everyone in the Mustangs' organization from the coaching staff on up, he wore his hair in a traditional cut, which, in her opinion, added to his sophisticated air.

"Alive. Barely." His deep voice was every bit as intoxicating as his excellent whiskey. Getting drunk on his words would be easy. Good thing he didn't talk much.

She rose up on her elbows as he shifted to his knees, facing her. Lord, he was handsome—and way out of her league. She attracted her fair share of nice-looking guys, but they'd all been baby-faced boys, playing at being men compared to Jake. Instead of making him look old, the lines on his face added character. Looking into his eyes, she got the feeling he'd experienced far more than anyone knew. There were secrets buried beneath those blue lakes.

Whatever those secrets were, they hadn't prevented him from enjoying life. Laugh lines radiated from the corners of his eyes, highlighting the smile breaking across his face.

"My turn. Take the dress off. I want to see you."

She lifted the flimsy garment over her head, dropping it to the floor. Her nipples tightened to hard peaks under his scrutiny.

"Beautiful." He weighed her breasts in his palms. His thumbs stroked the aching nubs, sending jolts of electricity to her pussy. She groaned, arching into his touch.

Reaching for the glass on the nightstand, he brought it to his lips. He took a sip, swallowed then sipped again. He swirled the last around in his mouth before swallowing it down, too. She almost came off the bed when he sucked her left breast into his mouth. The whiskey burned, but it was his tongue igniting an entirely different fire that did her in. Wrapping her arms around his head, she held him fast.

"Like that?" he asked, taking another swig from the glass.

"Mmm." *Yes. Oh my God, yes.*

He gave the other breast the same thorough attention. Fire licked her insides, stealing her inhibitions. She moaned and writhed, holding his head close. When he released her nipple then sat back on his heels, she closed her eyes. A groan slipped past her lips.

"Not done yet, sweetheart."

Thank God.

His hands closed over her ankles, slid up to her knees. Slipping beneath her legs, he caressed the sensitive skin where her legs hinged. Applying insistent pressure, he lifted, spreading her thighs wide. She flung her hands behind her to keep from toppling over.

When he fixed his gaze on her pussy, a thrill shot through her body. No one had ever looked at her the way he was— like he'd been wandering in the desert for a week and she was a fresh-water spring.

"Don't move." He reached for the tumbler, filled his mouth with the fiery elixir. Clenching the comforter in both fists, she watched as he lowered his head between her legs. His open mouth pressed to her swollen flesh ignited a wildfire. Flames radiated from her core to the tips of her extremities.

"Jake! Oh my God!"

Collapsing onto the bed, she closed her eyes in order to focus inward. The man had skills. Whiskey, whiskers, and the flat of his tongue conspired to scramble what little sanity his teeth and lips didn't obliterate. He knew things about her anatomy she didn't. He knew when to be gentle, where being a bit rough would add an edge to her pleasure.

Desperate for release, she arched her

back in an effort to get closer to the source of the unrelenting pleasure. She would have closed her legs around him, trapped him to her, if he hadn't held her legs in his iron grip. With each stroke of his tongue, each nip of his teeth, each caress of his lips, he wound the coil of tension inside her until she quivered like a bowstring drawn tight.

"Please." Her mouth formed the word, but she couldn't be sure the sound passed her lips. Everything within her was tuned to one spot low in her abdomen where pain of denied pleasure threatened to consume her.

Her plea might have reached his ears, she'd never know. Without breaking contact, he shoved her legs higher, tilting her ass in the air. He leaned into her, devouring her like she was the last thing he'd taste on earth. Sounds vibrated through his lips to her pussy, words she couldn't comprehend.

She stilled—a moment frozen in time as if her body stood on a precipice between two equal chasms. On one side was death. On the other, life so brilliant it blinded. For a heartbeat, she hovered over the crater of death. He moved his mouth against her. She felt rather than heard his command. Come.

So simple. So pure. So right. His voice tugged at her consciousness. She swayed away from death toward the brilliance of life. The lock imprisoning her pleasure snapped. She was free-falling toward the light. Pleasure so sharp it wounded, wracked her body.

Tears of joy spilled from her eyes as wave after wave of ecstasy carried her on invisible currents.

She was safe. Strong arms held her, protected her from crashing to the bottom. As the first headlong rush eased to a gentle soaring, she dared to open her eyes.

"Jake," she breathed.

He smiled down at her—a beautiful, triumphant smile she answered with a weak one of her own.

"You are so damn beautiful."

She was mush. A big puddle of sexually satisfied goo. He lifted her easily, sliding her up on the bed. In a moment, he sheathed himself. He moved over her, his cock stretching her, filling her, completing her.

When he was as deep as he could go, he paused, looking down at her. His eyes mirrored everything she felt. Wonder. Lust. Fear. Love.

He began to move inside her. His eyelids dropped, denying the feelings she'd seen so clearly in his eyes. Her pussy grasped at his cock in a vain attempt to bind him to her. He wouldn't be imprisoned. Retreating then thrusting hard, he repeatedly dared her to claim him.

Her heart cried out for its answering beat, though she could hear it, there was no answer. He'd shuttered himself away from her.

Relentlessly, his body demanded a response from hers. As much as she wanted to scream, to plead for him to give as much as he was asking, she was powerless when it came to her own body. He demanded she give him all. She gave him everything. She gave her body, her heart, her soul.

Her second orgasm was nothing the first one had been. Instead of feeling loved and cherished like before, this time she felt alone and forsaken.

As he took his own pleasure from her, tears came again—not for her loss, but for his. She'd glimpsed what could be between them. She was ready to embrace it, would have walked into the future with him without any doubts, but he'd shut that door with an unshakable finality.

When the last shudders of his orgasm subsided, she shoved against his shoulders until he rolled away from her. She ran to the adjoining bathroom. Slamming the door, she sank to the floor—a trembling mass of misery.

CHAPTER SIX

Present - Thanksgiving
Day

"You okay?" Her brother's deep voice nearby brought her back to reality.

Siobhan nodded, scooting over on the sofa so there would be room for him, too. She would rather barricade herself in the small pool house out back of Bentley Randolph's house than sit on the man's sofa and pretend to be cheerful. Sean, however, had all but dragged her across the backyard earlier.

"I'm fine." Only an idiot would have believed her sincere. "Is it too early for me to go back to my place?"

Sean covered her clasped hands with one of his. "Don't you want to spend Thanksgiving with family?"

Since they hadn't invited Sean, she'd turned down the invitation from her and Sean's blood family in order to spend the holiday with her brother's new family, whom, by extension, were hers, too. Not everyone in attendance knew about or understood the unorthodox relationship he shared with Bentley and Ashley, but none questioned the quirky dynamic either. For that, she was thankful.

"You know I do. But it's not easy being around all these cheerful people."

The guests consisted of a few of Bent and Ashley's relatives mixed with some co-workers Sean and Ashley knew from the TV network where they both worked. Her brother looked relaxed, but she could see the unease in his eyes. They all walked a fine line—trying to appear to be casual friends when in fact the three of them shared a bed. Today's gathering was a test of sorts for them to see if they could pull it off. She was certain they could, if they would all relax, quit looking as if they were guilty of something.

"Cheerful? Do I look cheerful to you? If Bentley gets any more cheerful, the stick he has up his ass is going to snap in two."

"Shh!" She ducked her head to conceal her laughter. "I don't think your guests have noticed, so don't bring it to their attention."

"I don't see how they could miss the tension." He turned to look at her. "Please, don't leave me here alone with these people."

The exaggerated pleading expression on his face lightened her mood. Chuckling, she shook her head. "Since you put it that way...I'll stay."

He patted her hand then stood to smile down at her. "Cowboys are on. Want to come into the den to watch the game?"

"I will in a minute. I've been sitting here feeling sorry for myself long enough.

I should go see if I can help in the kitchen."

She found Ashley alone in the kitchen "Where did everyone go?"

"To watch the game, I think." She glanced up from stirring the contents of the big bowl in front of her. "Why aren't you in there?"

Siobhan shrugged. "I came to see if you needed any help, and I wanted to talk to you."

Her hostess dropped the spoon in the bowl before reaching for a towel. "I've been hoping for a chance to talk to you, too." She wiped her hands clean as she crossed to the fridge. Pulling two plastic bottles from the massive Sub-Zero unit, she held one out to Siobhan.

"Water?"

"Sure, thanks."

Ashley claimed the stool next to hers.

"What did you want to talk to me about?"

Her friend took a long drink from her water bottle. Setting it aside, her hostess turned to face her. "I wanted to thank you for stepping into my shoes for the Crystal Ball. I'm up to my eyeballs with events to plan. Having that one off my list of worries is a godsend."

Siobhan swallowed the words she wanted to say. No matter how messed up her life was, the genuine gratitude on her friend's face prevented her from dumping her emotional baggage the way she'd planned. "No worries. You did most of the work. All I have to do is follow up on a few things."

Deep lines formed between Ashley's eyebrows. "You aren't mad at me?"

She was, but there was no use holding onto the feeling. Her intentions had been pure, if not misguided. "No. But, it's not going to work. Jake and I are through."

"I'm so sorry." She wrapped Siobhan in a big hug. "I thought maybe…if you saw each other again."

Siobhan stiffened, pushing away from the embrace. "We saw each other. I can assure you, nothing has changed."

"What happened?"

"He told me I was nothing more than a good…well, you know."

"No!" Ashley straightened, squaring

her shoulders. "I'm going to kill him!" She laid her hand over Siobhan's forearm. "I'm so, so sorry. He asked me to set something up so he could talk to you. He told me he'd screwed up. All he wanted was a chance to get back together with you, but you weren't answering his calls or emails. You have to believe me. I never would have set this up if I'd known he would do something like that to you."

"I know you wouldn't have." She took a sip from the water she'd all but ignored. Ashley's words sank in. But...wait. Are you saying Jake asked you to set us up?"

Ashley nodded. "That's exactly what I'm saying." Crossing her arms on the bar, she bent to rest her head on them. "I can't believe I fell for his sob story."

Siobhan thought about the new information while she patted her friend on the back. Why in the world would Jake go to the trouble of setting up a meeting just to insult her?

Her friend sat up. "I'm sorry, Siobhan. He sounded so...sincere."

"It's not your fault. Really, it isn't. Jake and I...well, we seem to know what buttons to push."

"I don't get it." Ashley dabbed at her watery eyes with a paper napkin. "Why go to the trouble of asking me to help him? Why contact you at all?"

"I'm wondering the same thing. When he broke it off last month, there was no ambiguity. He wanted out." God, she hated remembering that night. The pain of his parting words still had the power to make her physically ache.

"I just don't get it. The way he talked...he fessed up to ending things badly with you. He sounded sincere about wanting another chance. He *said* he loved you."

Siobhan shivered, shaking off the implications of her friend's words. "He doesn't know what love is—"

A roar from the crowd in the den jolted her out of her musings.

Today was a celebration. She had no right to drag it down with tales of her miserable love life. "Enough about Jake. Maybe he'll slink back to wherever he's been for the last month. If he does, I'll take over Bentley's share of responsibilities, too." She stood, drawing

Ashley into a hug. "Don't worry about me. I'll be fine."

"I can't tell you how sorry I am."

"No. No more apologies." She surveyed the controlled chaos in the kitchen. "I'm getting hungry, so let's get this show on the road before the football game goes to halftime. What can I do to help?"

Ashley pointed to the chopping board piled high with fruit. "If you really want to help, you can begin there. Fruit salad for ten."

Groaning, Siobhan transferred to the stool nearer her assigned task. It hadn't been long since she'd occupied the same stool. A few short months since she and her brother had sat at this same counter talking.

CHAPTER SEVEN

Two months earlier -

September 25th

"There isn't room for both of us in the pool house." Siobhan stared at her brother across the granite-topped island in Bentley's kitchen, afraid she knew where Sean was going with his suggestion. She wasn't blind or stupid.

"I know. We'll be changing places.

You'll have the pool house all to yourself for as long as you want to remain in Dallas. I'll be moving in here—with Ashley and Bent."

With the heels of her hands pressed into the edge of the counter, she drummed her fingers on the cold stone. *That's what I was afraid of.* She sighed. "Do you know what you're doing?"

He nodded his dark head. "I do. I love Bentley, and he loves me. Do I wish I was the only one he loved? Yes. But he loves Ashley, too. I can live with that if she can live with him loving me." He shrugged. "It's complicated."

"That's an understatement if I ever heard one." She'd known her older brother was gay for years but loved him just the same. All she'd ever wanted was for him to be happy. Even though his career in baseball was over, she'd never seen him as happy as he'd been the last few weeks. He'd recently signed a broadcasting contract to host a live, syndicated sports talk show that would provide him with financial security for years to come. Sean was the perfect host for the show, but she still worried about his adjustment to life post baseball. His jumping into a non-traditional, personal relationship added to her concerns.

"Will you do it?" he asked.

"You know I will, but are you sure you want to do this? I like to think I'm open-minded about sexual relationships, but when it comes to family, I find I lean toward traditional."

"Sis, there's no such thing as traditional where I'm concerned. I can't walk away from Bentley. We've already spent five years denying what we feel for each other. I don't want to waste another day—even if I have to share his affections with Ashley."

"She's okay with you moving in?"

"She's the one who suggested it." He smiled. "She's an incredible woman."

"I know. I've had a chance to get to know her over the last few months. I like her, too. I just don't want you getting hurt, Sean."

"There aren't guarantees in any relationship. This one is working, for the time being. I'd regret it the rest of my life if I didn't give it a chance."

She nodded. "Okay. Okay. I'll move

out to the pool house today, so you and your lovers can have the run of the house without your little sister cramping your style."

"Thanks. You were always my favorite sister."

"You're my favorite brother."

They both laughed at their joke. They didn't have any other siblings. Sean's laughter died away. The somber expression replacing his smile made her want to bolt for the door. She could see it coming—the big brother lecture.

"I'm worried about you, sis."

They'd had this conversation before regarding the man she was dating. She hadn't appreciated it much at the time, but after several weeks spent in Jake's bed, she could see where her brother might have valid concerns. She had a few herself.

"I'm good, Sean. I'm being cautious."

"He never keeps a girlfriend during the off season. Everyone says he disappears as soon as the season is over. It's like he vanishes until Spring Training. I don't know what to make of his habits, but whatever he does for those months, he doesn't want anyone to know."

She'd heard about Jake's tendency to dump his girlfriends at the end of the season, but she hadn't heard the bit about him going MIA for months. "Where did you hear that? The locker room?"

"As a matter of fact, yes. I made it a point to ask a few questions last week when I went to clean out my locker and say my goodbyes to the team."

She frowned at his admission.

"Don't be mad at me. What kind of big brother would I be if I didn't look out for you?"

"The kind that doesn't meddle in his sister's business?"

"You can call it meddling if you want, but I call it protecting. You said you don't want me getting hurt, well, I don't want you getting hurt either. Knowledge is power. I figure you're going to need all the knowledge you can get in regards to Jake."

"I can take care of myself." She wasn't going to tell her brother, but the new information did have her wondering what Jake was hiding.

"I think you should go back to D.C. I'm glad you came out to help me after the accident, but I'm fine. The hip is about as good as it's ever going to get, I have a new job, and I'm going to be living with the man I love. Go home before Jake breaks your heart."

Too late for that. Jake had stomped all over her heart their first night together, but like a lovesick idiot, she continued to hope she could reach the part of him she'd glimpsed the first time they made love.

"I can't, Sean. I promised Ashley I would stay until after their wedding."

"Don't remind me about the wedding." He grimaced. "I still can't believe I'm going to be the Best Man."

Her heart softened. She couldn't imagine how difficult it would be for him to stand up for Bentley when he would prefer to be exchanging vows with the man. "You don't have to do it."

"Yeah, I do." His shoulders slumped. "They both have to maintain their public images. Getting married will make everything seem normal surrounding them. Only a few people, like you, need to know what's really going on between us."

She was sorry her brother carried such a heavy burden in order to be with the man he loved, but she was grateful the conversation had turned away from her.

"You know I'm always here for you."

"I know. I appreciate it." He stood, a big smile spreading across his face. "Come on. I don't have much, but I could use some help getting my stuff over here. I'll help you take your stuff to the pool house afterward. You're coming with me to the game this afternoon, aren't you?"

She followed her brother out the back door, falling into step beside him. "I wouldn't miss the first playoff game." She tried to keep her voice casual so he wouldn't suspect she had other reasons for attending. "I wish you were playing, but I'm glad the Mustangs made it this far."

"You know, I haven't watched a Major League game from the stands since I was in high school."

"We're in the owner's skybox, aren't

we?"

"Yep."

"Today's experience will be a whole lot better than the outfield seats we used to get."

"Those were fun times." Sean draped his arm over her shoulder. "I'd buy season tickets in the outfield if there were such a thing."

She smiled, remembering how much enjoyment they'd gotten out of the cheapest seats in the stadium. "Me, too. I suspect you have other reasons for liking the outfield these days."

He chuckled. "Yeah, left field is a lot more interesting than it used to be."

She rolled her eyes. "That's what I thought. Bentley does have a fine ass."

"Hey!"

"Don't worry. He's not my type." She sped up to outdistance him on the sidewalk. "Let's hurry and get the moving done. I want to see batting practice before the game."

CHAPTER EIGHT

Present - December 2nd

"You don't need to be here. I can handle this." Siobhan tapped her foot on the sidewalk outside the downtown hotel where the Crystal Ball would take place.

"I know you can handle it, but there's no reason you should have to handle it alone," Jake said. "I signed on to do my part, too."

The man could be so exasperating.

"This isn't your part."

"That's because Ashley is a control freak. She insisted on doing her tasks as well as Bentley's. According to the stuff Bent gave me, dealing with the ballroom issues was his job."

She glared up at him. For the millionth time wondered exactly why he was in Dallas, plaguing her. "Like I said, I don't need you." Turning, she headed for the revolving door a few steps away. She paused, waiting for a couple to exit so she could slip into the vacated compartment. Jake's voice, low and seductive just over her shoulder, sent shivers down her back.

"I need you."

His breath hot against her ear was like dropping a pebble in a calm lake. Ripples of lust radiated out from her lobe all the way to the tips of her fingers. Lord, he could still make her knees weak. But she was made of sterner stuff than when she'd first met him. She'd already had that disease. Once a woman lived through a bout of Jake Tulleson, she was immune to his seduction.

The door swished past, revealing an empty stall. She waited a heartbeat. At the last second, she stepped in, leaving heartbreak behind.

"Fuck." Jake watched the spinning compartment until it reached the other side where it deposited Siobhan safely inside the hotel lobby. Her sure steps and swaying hips mesmerized him as she traversed the polished marble floor, releasing him when she turned a corner, disappearing down a connecting hallway.

He shook his head to clear it of erotic thoughts. No matter how many layers of clothing Siobhan wore, he could see through them like some fuckin' superhero. Only he was nobody's hero.

Zero. That's more like it.

A tour bus rumbled to a stop at the curb. A noisy group of teenagers poured out, jostling for position in front of the revolving door. Jake stepped back, allowing them room.

In his car, he cursed the midday traffic clogging the downtown streets. He didn't know what he'd expected when he returned, but this wasn't it. Yes, he'd been an ass, but he'd come back. He'd apologized. Hell, he'd done everything he could think of to win Siobhan over, but none of it had worked.

The satellite radio cut off, indicating an incoming call. He waited until the phone number appeared on the display before answering.

"Hi, hon. What's up?"

"I haven't heard from you all week, Dad. I hope you haven't called me because you've been in bed with Siobhan."

He stifled a groan. "I'm stuck in traffic, and my sleeping habits are none of your business," he chided. His daughter meant well, but he wasn't comfortable with her blunt approach to his love life.

"Oh, Dad," she sighed. "What did you do? I thought for sure she would have forgiven you by now."

"Shows what you know." Signaling a lane change, he looked over his shoulder before edging the car into the far right lane. "She hates me."

"I told you winning her back was going to take more than just showing up, but did you listen? No." She stretched the vowel sound out to emphasize her point. "You had to do it your way."

He resisted the urge to bear down on the horn. The traffic wasn't going anywhere, just like this conversation with his meddling daughter. "Look, Kelly, my love life, or lack thereof, is none of your business."

"I beg to differ, Daddy."

How the hell did she sound so mature yet so childish in the span of one sentence?

"You need her. She makes you happy, and when you're happy, so am I."

He couldn't argue with her logic. "Yes, she makes me happy but, apparently, I don't do the same for her. She just kicked me to the curb."

"So, what's next? You do have a plan, don't you?"

His silence condemned him. The long-suffering sigh Kelly had used to manipulate him since she was two years old put him on alert.

"Don't, Kel. I can hear the gears turning in your head from here. This is my problem, and I'm perfectly capable of solving it myself."

"You are so in denial. When's this dinner thing you're working on?"

"Weekend after next." He braked hard before he rear-ended the cement truck in front of him.

"Do you have a date?"

"I'm going with Siobhan."

"Really, Dad? The woman isn't speaking to you."

At a complete standstill on the LBJ Freeway, he closed his eyes long enough to say a silent prayer for patience. "That's only a temporary situation. She'll come around in time."

"You're going to win her over in ten days." She couldn't have infused more sarcasm into the statement if she'd tried.

"That's the plan." He clenched the steering wheel in a white-knuckled grip.

"Admit it. You don't have a plan."

"Okay." He poured all his frustration into the one word. "I don't have a plan, but I'll think of something."

"Admitting you have a problem is the first step to recovery."

When had his daughter developed such a smart mouth? "I don't have a problem," he reiterated.

"You do, too. Face it, Dad. It's time to make a call to the bullpen."

"This isn't a game, Kel. Besides, I don't have a bullpen."

"Yes, you do. Me."

He really didn't want to know what she meant by that, but he had little choice. Once his daughter grabbed onto a subject, she wouldn't let go. Just like the time she decided he needed to revamp his wardrobe. She'd been all of ten and certain she knew everything about men's fashions. He held off her good intentions for a week at best before driving her to the mall where she shoved armloads of clothes at him before sending him into the dressing room. Several thousand dollars later he had a new look he hadn't wanted, but in retrospect, he'd needed. But just because she was right about his closet didn't mean she was right about his love life. What did she know about the complicated relationships between men and women?

"Kel," he warned.

"I'm coming down there, Dad. I'll book my ticket as soon as we hang up. Can you pick me up at the airport tomorrow?"

He knew when he was defeated.

"Text me with your flight information. I'll be there."

She did that squeal thing she did whenever she got her way, which was more often than he cared to think about. He'd been a mostly absent parent but, he reasoned, he wouldn't have been there any more often if he'd married her mother all those years ago when they'd found out about the pregnancy. Major League baseball players were on the road more than they were home. It was a fact of life he'd compensated for in the off-season by indulging his daughter, perhaps a bit too much. All things considered, Kelly had turned out okay.

They ended the call with a game of *I love you, I love you more,* that made him forget he was supposed to be annoyed with her.

By the time he pulled into his driveway, he'd come to the conclusion that perhaps Kelly was right. He needed help. It just sucked he was reduced to relying on his daughter who wasn't much younger than the woman he was in love with. It only made the age-divide seem wider, more impossible to span. He so didn't want to think about what his daughter knew about adult relationships. She was too young....

Shit.

CHAPTER NINE

Two months earlier -

September 25th

Jake turned off his cell phone. He'd made sure the house in Colorado would be fit to live in when he arrived. The couple he paid to watch it for him was always easy about his uncertain arrival dates. As long as he gave them a heads-up a few weeks in advance, they'd sweep the cobwebs out, have the chimneys cleaned, as well as make sure the appliances were in working order. This year, he asked them to order more firewood. The stack had been getting low when he'd left in February.

There wasn't much he liked more than a real wood fire in the fireplace. His house in Dallas had a fake fireplace. Who'd ever heard of a remote control fire? It was useless for anything but looking at. *Might as well have one of those TV screensavers of a burning fireplace.*

Everything was set. All he needed to do was get through the post-season then he'd get to go home to the love of his life.

The Mustangs team looked good on paper, but they'd lost one good man in the lineup when Sean Flannery took his swan dive into the dugout late in the season. His replacement, a kid brought up from the minors, was eager to prove himself, which was the rookie's main problem. He was too eager. So far, nothing Jake told him about having patience when he was at the plate had sunk in. He'd seen it a million times but, just once, he wished for a rookie who'd been broken to the saddle before they trotted him out for the show.

After a quick change into his uniform, he stepped out of his office. A crowd of players in their warm-up uniforms blocked the hallway leading to the dugout. They all laughed together over something he was too far away to hear. He smiled. As part of the coaching staff, his responsibility, as he saw it, was to keep moral up. A team in good spirits generally played better than if the mood was somber. As he got closer, he began to pick out individual voices. The usual suspects were in attendance—the jokesters of the roster plus a few others he trusted to keep things from getting out of hand. Jason Holder was as nice a guy as they came, but a stickler for the rules. Singling his voice out, even before he could see his head in the crowd, Jake knew the gathering was under control.

He approached, hoping to skirt the group without anyone noticing. No need for him to put an end to their fun. Jason would see they all made it out to the field on time.

"Thanks for all your help." A voice

from the center of the crowd stopped Jake. His pulse kicked up, his dick following suit. *Siobhan. What's she doing here?*

"I've got to get back up to our box before Sean sends a search party out for me. Can't have him ruining the surprise."

Surprise? Oh yeah. The pre-game program.

The players filed away, each one calling out his best wishes until only the two people in the center remained. Jason Holder and Siobhan Flannery.

"You know your way out?" Jason asked her.

"I'll make sure she gets back where she needs to be." He stepped forward, addressing Jason. "If anyone is looking for me, tell them I'll be out in a few minutes."

"Sure thing." Jason waved goodbye to Siobhan as he headed toward the dugout.

"Everything is set?" Jake asked since his brain wasn't capable of coming up with anything cleverer. He'd heard talk about today's opening ceremonies and the tribute to her brother's years in the game. Since the Mustangs were playing the

Pioneers—the team Sean had played for the longest during his career—the timing seemed logical. It was Siobhan's job to get her brother down to the field at the appropriate time. Nothing like throwing a surprise party with forty thousand guests.

"I think so." She turned, heading toward the bank of elevators that would take her back up to the owner's box. "Sean was excited about coming to the stadium, but I don't think he has a clue he's the pre-game entertainment."

Jake fell into step with her. "Your brother deserves the recognition. He's made a real contribution over the years."

She pushed the elevator call button before turning to smile at him. "Thanks, Jake. Leaving baseball has been difficult for him, even with the broadcasting job he's lined up. I think he would rather have left because he was too old to play."

"That's the way we all want to go out. I know how he feels. My knees gave out long before I was ready to hang it up."

Sympathy softened her gaze. "I didn't know."

"Don't feel sorry for me. I found a

way to stay in the game. It sounds as if Sean has, too. I'd be happy to talk to him, if you think it might help."

"I appreciate your offer, Jake. I'll let you know if he starts to feel sorry for himself." She placed her palm over his cheek. "You're a good man."

Her flowery scent was such a contrast to the stale sweat odor permeating everything in the clubhouse, he yearned to get closer. She was so good—literally a breath of fresh air.

"I admire your dedication to your brother," he said.

Their gazes locked. He'd seen that look in her eyes every time he'd taken her to his bed—invitation, longing. The elevator dinged its arrival. She stepped away, taking her hand with her. When the doors opened, he followed her into the small cubicle.

She pressed a button on the control panel. "Don't you have someplace to be?"

"Probably." He couldn't remember. All he knew was he needed to be here, with her. "I don't know. I don't care."

Her eyes widened as he advanced on her. The clipboard he'd been holding like a lifeline dropped to the floor. One hand wrapped around her waist, pulling her lower body against his while the other captured her nape. Her lips parted on a surprised gasp. Taking that as an invitation, he swooped in. Her eyes zeroed in on his mouth—her lashes fanning across her cheeks as he closed the distance between them.

Electricity sparked when their bodies met, setting fire to his blood. God, she tasted even better than she smelled. He couldn't get enough of her, and Lord, he'd tried over the last few weeks.

She melted against him for the few seconds it took for the car to rise to her floor. When it jolted to a stop, he quickly reached out, jabbing his finger against the button to keep the doors from opening. They both needed a minute to recover.

His dick was at full attention. Her lips were the tantalizing color of ripe plums. He briefly considered dragging her off somewhere to finish what he'd begun, but reason prevailed. The memory of the flush he'd put on her cheeks would have to do for until he could finish what he'd started. This was not the time or the place for the kind of things running through his mind.

"Tonight."

She nodded, straightening her clothes. "Yes."

Releasing the button, he reclaimed his clipboard, putting a respectable distance between them just as the doors opened. She stepped out without so much as a backward glance, her perfect round ass swaying with each step.

Shit. Every time he was with her, he swore to himself it would be the last. He should have let her go after their first night, but when he heard her crying in the bathroom, he'd known he couldn't let her leave believing he was an ass—even if it was true. For some reason, he wanted her to think better of him. He'd patiently coaxed her out and taken her back to bed, where he'd spent the rest of the evening trying to undo the damage he'd done.

He hadn't been entirely successful. Though she'd come to his bed every night the team was in town since that first time, he sensed she came for the physical gratification alone. That first night, she'd gotten under his skin with her openness, her need to be with him. He'd wanted sex with a woman he desired but, with Siobhan, the physical connection had been only a small part of what he'd felt. She'd broken down the barriers he'd spent years building, and in the seconds it took him to put the barriers back up, she'd seen too much.

It scared the hell out of him to think he'd allowed her to get so close. He'd spent two decades fortifying his defenses, but the minute he'd dipped his dick in Siobhan's heat, the walls around his heart began to crumble.

The breakdown lasted a few seconds, at most, before he'd shut her out. She was different from any female he'd ever been with. She made him want something beyond the season. But that wouldn't happen. He'd known since he signed his first Minor League contract he wasn't a relationship kind of guy.

Mercy! If she wasn't careful, the fire Jake stoked in her would consume her. She'd managed to get through the opening ceremonies, pulling off the surprise for her brother completely. He hadn't suspected a thing until the last minute when she'd had to tell him what was going on in order to get him into the elevator.

The large contingent that accompanied them to the suite was doing serious damage to the buffet and open bar at the back the room, which left her alone to watch the game, which also meant she had plenty of time to contemplate the mess she'd gotten herself into.

She continued to tell herself there was nothing more than sex between her and Jake, but it hadn't been the truth from the beginning. Whatever they had, it had flared bright for all of two seconds before Jake brought the shutters down on it. Those two seconds changed her life. She'd seen what a real relationship could be.

Her heart still ached at the memory of how much it hurt when he'd shut her out. Sitting on his bathroom floor, she'd thought she might die from the pain. She should have demanded he take her home instead of crawling back into his bed, but she'd hoped he would open up to her again—let her see what he was feeling one more time.

Stupid. He'd had decades to practice hiding his feelings. Taking a page from his book, she put walls around the love growing inside her, so he wouldn't see while she gave her body to him. He was a skilled lover, just as she'd imagined he would be. What she learned in his bed was already making a difference in her writing.

You wanted to spice up your bedroom scenes. You should be grateful for the lessons.

She was grateful, but as each day passed, she worried the price she would have to pay for her tutoring would be higher than she could ever have imagined.

He'll discard you as soon as the season is over.

Sean had warned her. At the time, a few months of wild, wicked sex with Jake, no strings or rings attached, had been exactly what she was looking for.

A large hand on her shoulder startled her. "Everything all right?" Sean dropped into the seat beside her, propping his booted feet on the low, glass-topped wall. He handed her one of the two beer bottles he carried.

She smiled to hide her inner turmoil. "I'm fine. The game is going well."

"Yep. Looks like."

"Are *you* okay? I can't imagine what it's like for you to watch this instead of play."

He took a long swig from his beer. "Better than I thought I would be. I knew I wasn't going back to baseball, but the pre-game thing really hammered it home for me. I was pissed at first that the ceremony was sprung on me like it was, but if I'd known about it beforehand, I probably would have refused to come. That would have been a shame. I needed the closure, and I didn't even know it."

"I'm glad it worked out. I felt awful about not telling you."

"I hope you lost sleep over it." He smiled. "Don't think I'll forget either."

"You mean it, don't you? You are ready to move on."

"Darn right he is." Bentley Randolph's fiancée, Ashley, shuffled into the row of seats behind them. She'd been part of the ceremony earlier, introducing Sean as the new anchor for the syndicated sports talk show, *Around the League*. "The network has big plans for your brother."

"I wasn't so sure the plans he'd made were right for him," Siobhan told the other woman, "but it looks like he's going to be fine. The best thing about his new job is he won't be breaking any more bones. I think he might have reached the limit on reconstructive surgery."

"Amen to that," Sean said. "At the rate I was injuring myself, I was going to be a cripple in another year or two. As long as I don't fall out of my chair on set, I should be able to walk myself into a nursing home in about fifty years or so."

"Sounds like a plan to me." Ashley leaned forward. "How's our boy doing?" she asked Sean, referring to the man they both loved, Bentley Randolph, the Mustangs left fielder.

"I haven't seen much of the game yet." He pointed toward the Mustangs dugout. "He looks fine though."

Siobhan looked toward the dugout. Bentley stood on the steps, one foot on the tread above the other, his bat in one hand, helmet in the other.

"Yum yum," Ashley said. "He looks

good enough to eat."

"He always does," her brother mumbled, so only the three of them could hear.

The two of them continued to exchange inappropriate comments regarding their lover. They could drool all they wanted over Bentley, her eyes were for the man who had joined him. Jake, clipboard in hand, was imparting some kind of information to the left fielder before he made his way to the on-deck circle.

Standing in the dugout during the pre-game ceremonies, watching Sean's friends on both teams congratulate him on his career, wishing him well in the future, she'd been aware of Jake's perusal. The kiss in the elevator had been risky—not to mention, he was supposed to have been on the field, making sure the Mustangs were all in top form for the game.

What had it meant? It was an unspoken rule that their affair was private. They didn't go around in public at all. She supposed the fewer people who knew about a relationship, the easier it would be to end it. There'd be no explanations needed to the press or mutual friends. Sean would be the least surprised.

That left Bent and Ashley. Bent wouldn't be any more surprised than Sean Ashley would be sympathetic, but she had her hands full planning her wedding. She wouldn't want to dwell on Siobhan's pathetic love life any longer than necessary.

On the field, Bentley took his turn at bat. Whatever Jake had told him to do, it worked. He connected with the second pitch, sending the ball over the left field wall for a two-run homer. Siobhan jumped to her feet, shouting along with everyone else in the box. The Mustangs needed to win this series in order to continue in the playoffs. If she had her way about it, they'd make it all the way to the World Series, preferably dragging it out to the seventh game. She wanted every minute she could get with Jake before he disappeared to wherever it was he went during the off-season.

CHAPTER TEN

Present - December 8th

He'd lain awake the night before, trying to devise a plan of his own to get past the barriers Siobhan had put up, but as he stood in the crowded terminal at DFW, watching the people on the descending escalator, he knew he was up the proverbial creek without a paddle. He had nothing. Nada. Zip.

After a week of being summarily

told to go back to the rock he'd climbed out from under, he had to admit, Kelly might be his best, if not his only, chance. He still couldn't think of his daughter as grown up, and he damned sure didn't want to dwell on the fact she might have more in common with the woman he loved than he did. But, again, he knew when he was defeated. Kelly was right. It was time to call the bullpen.

A new throng of travelers discharged from the upper floor of the terminal into the crowd of people waiting for friends and loved ones. He didn't want to contemplate what the last minute ticket had cost him, but as soon as he saw his daughter's face, he knew the purchase was worth it.

Tears distorted his vision as she ran to where he waited. "God, I've missed you." He wrapped her in his arms. The top of her head fit under his chin. When had she gotten so tall? Even through the layers of clothes, it was obvious she wasn't the little girl he wanted to believe she was. She'd grown up when he wasn't looking.

"I missed you, too." Grabbing him

by the hand, she tugged him toward the baggage carousel. "Let's get my stuff. I'll tell you my plan on the way to your house."

His house. Not home. She'd never been to the residence he kept in Dallas. It was little more than a stopping off place for him during the season. Since Kelly's mother preferred her daughter lead a stable life, he'd gone to see her when he could, instead of her coming to him. Very few people in the League even knew he had a daughter. His private life was just that—private.

He pushed the cart loaded down with luggage across the busy traffic lanes to the parking garage. "Are you visiting or moving in?" he asked, cramming the extra bags that wouldn't fit in the sports car's miniature trunk into the backseat.

"Visiting. But you never know. It might take a while to resolve this thing with Siobhan. If my plan works, I'll be out of your hair next week."

She didn't have to fill in the blanks. If her plan didn't work, she was prepared to lay siege to his love life, using his house as her base camp for the duration.

"So, tell me about this idea of yours." He cranked the ignition. Stalling for time, he adjusted the vents to warm her side of the car, too, figuring he'd be better off hearing her plan while the vehicle was safely parked.

"Okay." She turned sideways in the seat, tucking her left leg under her right. Her eyes sparkled with purpose—a sure sign she was hell bent on carrying out her scheme. He'd seen the look before. "Siobhan loves you, but you fu…screwed up, so now she says she hates you."

He sighed, scanned the parking lot rather than let her see how much her blunt recap hurt. "Yeah, that about sums it up."

"It's simple, really. All you have to do is make her jealous. Show up at this dinner thing, ball, whatever, with another woman. Act like you got the message. Make her think you've moved on."

Terror struck him right in the heart. No way was he going to ask another woman to the Crystal Ball. He'd go alone or not at all before he'd ask someone else. A date to an event of that caliber came with expectations afterward.

"No way in hell." He put the car in reverse. "I'm not taking some random date to the ball in order to make Siobhan jealous."

"I know." Kelly practically bounced in her seat. "I never said you had to take a random woman. That's why I'm here. I'll be your date."

Tires screeched as he brought the big cat to a stop in the middle of the aisle. "What?" he bellowed.

"You heard me. I'll be your date. No one knows me here. Even if you've been showing my photo around, not a soul would recognize me. Last time I looked, you still had my picture from eighth grade in your wallet."

He could feel his neck turning red as the barb struck home. The photo she referred to was one of his favorites, and he'd seen no reason to replace it. "Kelly—"

"You better drive. I think the person behind us wants our parking spot."

A quick check in the rearview mirror confirmed the impatient driver behind them. He pressed the accelerator. After paying to exit the lot, he resumed the conversation. "I'm not taking you to the ball."

"Have you got a better idea?"

He merged onto the freeway dividing the facility in half. A few minutes later, when he paid the toll to exit the airport, he was no closer to proving Kelly wrong than he had been the day before. He didn't have shit in the way of an idea, much less a plan.

"Want to go to a ball with me?" he asked with a grin.

CHAPTER ELEVEN

Present - December 10th

The last place on earth Siobhan wanted to be was at a ball, but there was no way around it. When she'd agreed to take over the responsibilities on the planning committee, she'd signed on for attending as well. *I'm such a fraud. All I did was follow up with a few vendors, answer some questions, make a couple of phone calls.* The sum total of her contribution was minimal, making Ashley and Bent's interference in her life all the more obvious.

She sighed. *Water under the bridge.* Devious as their plan had been, it hadn't worked. She'd managed to thwart Jake's every move. When he'd first started showing up to help her with the various tasks assigned to her, she'd sent him packing with sharp words and a don't-fuck-with-me attitude. He must have gotten the message she was serious about not wanting to see him again because, in the week leading up to the ball, the unsolicited visits ceased.

Maybe he crawled back under his rock.

"Is everything all right?" Her brother's hand on the small of her back was reassuring. At least she hadn't been forced to come alone. Sean hated the vintage Captain Kirk costume Bentley had intended to wear, but it fit him perfectly, the clinging fabric emphasizing his physique. She'd already noted several women checking him out.

"I'm fine. Just checking the table decorations. It appears the party supplier got it right, after all."

"Was there a problem?"

She nodded. "A small one, it seems. As of two weeks ago, they didn't have enough tall containers to do centerpieces on all the tables. It didn't take a genius to solve the problem by alternating with the shorter ones."

"Looking good."

"You'd say that no matter what," she teased.

"I wasn't talking about the room. I was talking about you. You look like a million bucks."

She was wearing the dress Ashley purchased for the event. Once she'd decided not to attend, she'd insisted on Siobhan making use of the gown. The silver beaded, halter-style garment had a high-banded neck that fell away, leaving her back exposed down to the swell of her hips. The one concession to this being a masquerade ball was the matching half-mask. Overall, the gown was sophisticated, expensive, and sexy. She'd never worn anything like it—probably never would again.

"I think Ashley may have spent about that much on this dress," she hedged.

"Worth every penny." Sean's hand slipped around her waist, steering her in the opposite direction. "What kind of flowers are those?" he asked, pointing at one of the floral arches positioned around the perimeter of the room.

A shiver ran down her spine. "He's here, isn't he?" she asked, knowing the answer was yes.

"We can go if you want to. I can make an excuse, say you're sick or something then I'll take you home."

"No. It's okay. We're adults. Besides, it's a big event. What are the chances of him even seeing me?"

Sean looked over his shoulder. "Pretty good, I'd say, sis."

"He saw us?" She pretended an interest in the flower arrangement her brother had asked about earlier.

"Yep." His arm tightened around her waist. "He's not alone, Siobhan."

She swallowed hard, willing her stomach to settle. She should be happy he'd moved on. That meant he had taken her message to heart.

It's what you wanted. So why did she

feel like crying?

"Flannery."

Jake's baritone tied her muscles in knots. Willing the crippling tension to leave her body, she turned, thankful for her brother's steadying arm around her waist.

Dear God. Her knees turned to jelly at the sight of the man who'd trampled her heart. Judging from the white dinner jacket and bow tie, he'd gone for the James Bond look. It worked. No on-screen Bond had anything on Jake Tulleson. He was testosterone in a tux, reducing her to a frumpy lump of female hormones. She felt herself swaying toward him, caught at the last minute by Sean's fingers digging into her skin.

"Jake." Her brother acknowledged the newcomer. "I heard you were back in town."

"I've been back a few weeks," he answered while his gaze raked her from head to toe. "Doing a favor for a friend."

"I heard." Sean's voice was cold. "Bent and Ashley are in over their heads these days."

She was drifting again.

Her brother brought her up tight against his side. "Who's this? I don't think I've had the pleasure."

Who? Siobhan blinked, breaking the spell Jake's arrival had cast over her. She followed her brother's gaze. Ice water replaced the heated blood flowing through her veins as she took in the woman at Jake's side. A baby. Younger even than she was. *Freakin' gorgeous.* The perfect Bond Girl to his 007. She wore the gold lame cat suit like a second skin over her long, coltish legs and athletic figure. The futuristic belt hanging low on her hips was her only adornment save the glittering gold on her eyelids and lips. About a yard of dark hair was caught up in a high ponytail draped over her shoulder. With one knee bent, her gold manicured fingers clung to her date's arm, so she fit against him like she'd been poured into a mold.

A toxic brew of emotions churned in Siobhan's gut. Disappointment. Jealousy. Hate. Love that refused to die even in the face of its executioner. She really was going to be sick. Sean wouldn't have to make anything up on her behalf.

"This is Kelly." He completed the introductions as smoothly as a secret agent on a mission.

Siobhan nodded at the younger woman who acknowledged the intro with a dazzlingly perfect smile.

"Are you okay?" Jake asked. His hand closing over her ice-cold fingers sent a blast of heat throughout her body. "You don't look so good."

He tugged her away from Sean. Over her shoulder, she silently implored her brother to rescue her, but the tawny cat had her claws in her brother, drawing him in the opposite direction. He gave her a helpless look before allowing Jake's date to whisk him off.

"I'm fine." She tried to brush Jake's hand away, but he was wrapped around her, hustling her toward the ballroom doors. She had no choice but to go along.

CHAPTER TWELVE

Present - December 10th.

It felt good to hold her again, like he'd gone to Heaven and found his angel. But something was seriously wrong. He wanted nothing more than for her to fall into his arms. Just not like this. When he first saw her across the glittering room, she'd sparkled brighter than all the rhinestones on her dress combined. But something happened while they were talking. Her face below the mask she wore lost all its color then she'd begun to sway like a twig in the wind.

Sean had caught her, held her upright, but damn her brother for not noticing something was really, *really* wrong. The Siobhan he knew and loved was made of sterner stuff than this.

He whisked her into the first elevator to arrive. She made no argument, just fell against him so he had no choice but to hold her. Placing one hand at the small of her back to support her, he noticed the light sheen of sweat on her skin. Panic gripped him around the throat.

"Babe," he croaked through dry lips. "Hang on. Just a few more minutes." No answer as he held her cheek against his lapel. *Shit. Maybe I should've called an ambulance. What do I know about anything medical?*

The elevator doors opened on his floor. He scooped her up, making his way down the hall as quick as he could without jostling her too much. At the door to the room he'd booked for the night, he fished the keycard out of his jacket pocket, slid it into the slot to release the lock.

She was out cold when he laid her on the bed. *Holy shit. What's wrong with her?*

"Siobhan, babe." Sitting beside her, he removed her mask. He cradled her face between his palms, stroking his thumbs over ashen cheeks. "Wake up, babe. Ah, Christ, sweetheart, you're scaring me."

What to do? He fumbled in his pocket for his cell phone, found Sean's number. "Get up here, now. Room 3425. It's Siobhan, she's sick."

His eyes blurred, but he managed to call the front desk. "I need a doctor up here. Fast. I don't care where you find one. Call 9-1-1 if you have to." He gave them the few details he knew, age, sex, that was it. Christ, he was useless. Why didn't he know more about her?

Because you're an ass, Tully.

Reaching for her hand, he held onto her, silently praying for her to open those gorgeous eyes of hers. Her skin was cold. God, he'd never seen a living person so pale. He pulled the comforter off the other side of the bed to cover her, tucking it in around her like a cocoon.

In the other room, a knock sounded on the door. He bolted to answer it. Sean Flannery pushed past him, followed by Kelly.

"Where is she?" he asked. Worry etched deep lines between his eyes and around his mouth. "What did you do to her, you bastard?"

"Nothing. She was sick down in the ballroom. What kind of brother are you? You didn't even notice!" He looked at his daughter. "I called for a doctor. Stay here, let him in." Signaling Sean to follow him to the bedroom, he called over his shoulder, "She's in here, asshole."

Fear gripped him. She was so pale— not at all the vibrant woman he remembered. Minutes later, Kelly escorted another woman into the room.

"I'm Dr. Simon." She took his place beside Siobhan.

She was quick and efficient, asking questions as she examined her patient. Between himself and Sean, they answered most of her questions, but it was her final inquiry that rocked him to the core.

"Is she pregnant?"

"No." He scraped the fingers of one hand through his hair as the possibility hit home. Fear was a fireball in his gut. *What if she is? It's mine.* He couldn't imagine she'd taken another lover after he left. She wasn't like that. They'd used protection, but nothing but abstinence was one hundred percent certain. They'd fucked like bunnies for weeks. "Maybe. Fuck, I don't know."

The doctor waved something under Siobhan's nose. Her moans were music to his ears as she came to.

"What happened?" she asked.

"You fainted." Dr. Simon, introduced herself. "Do you mind if I examine you?"

Confusion knitted Siobhan's brow as she scanned the room, landing on her audience before returning to the woman at her side. "No. But I'm fine...I think."

"Come on." Kelly waved both men into the other room. "Let's give them some privacy."

He wandered to the middle of the outer room where he stood, helpless. Lost. What if she was pregnant? He felt bad enough about the way he'd ended their relationship, but if she was carrying his child, he'd never forgive himself.

If he'd stayed…. She needed someone to take care of her. It should have been him.

The door closed behind them with a soft click. His daughter came to his side. "She'll be fine, Dad. You'll see."

Please, God. Please let her be okay.

"When was your last menstrual period?"

Siobhan's gaze flew from the blood pressure cuff wrapped around her arm to Dr. Simon's face. "Why?" She couldn't imagine what her cycle could have to do with anything.

The doctor removed the BP cuff, folding it neatly. "Because, there doesn't seem to be anything wrong with you. You're young, healthy, and I presume, in a sexual relationship with one of the men in the next room." Her words were kind rather than accusatory. "Is there a chance you could be pregnant?"

"No." She shook her head, trying to remember. "We used protection."

"Are you on the pill?"

A trickle of fear turned her blood to ice. "No. We were cautious. He always...."

"Condoms are not one hundred percent effective," she warned, pinning Siobhan with a serious expression. "Have you ever fainted before?"

"No."

"So, about that menstrual period?"

Now that she thought about it, she hadn't had one since before Jake left. "I've never been regular." Her mind scrambled, searching for any reason to dismiss the doctor's assumption.

"One month? Two?"

"Two. I think." Oh Lord. A pregnancy became more of a probability.

"Queasiness? Fatigue? Breast tenderness?"

Yes. Yes. Yes.

Dr. Simon took her hand in both of hers. "Look. I'm not the morality police here, but years of experience tell me the likelihood of you being pregnant is pretty high. Healthy women your age do not faint for no reason. You should visit your gynecologist sooner rather than later, just to make sure."

114

Unable to form words, she nodded.

Gathering her things, the other woman stood. She laid a white card on the nightstand. "Call me if you have any questions or if you need someone to talk to. I understand how overwhelming something like this can be."

Dr. Simon paused before opening the door. "Which one?" She tilted her head toward the closed door. "James Bond or Captain Kirk?"

Siobhan smiled for the first time since she'd woken up in the strange room. "James Bond. Captain Kirk is my brother."

The older woman pretended to swoon. "I thought so. Good genes. You'll make beautiful babies." She had a big smile on her face as she closed the door softly behind her.

Propped against the headboard, she tried to absorb what she knew to be true. She was pregnant. With Jake Tulleson's baby.

Her mind flitted all around but never once contemplated anything other than seeing the pregnancy through to a natural conclusion.

I'm having a baby.

Wonder and love blossomed in her heart, spreading warmth throughout her body. She placed her hands over her stomach, willing the life inside to feel her love. She didn't have a clue how to be a mother, but she'd learn. Daddy or no, her child was going to be loved.

Daddy. Jake.

As if her thoughts conjured him up, the door opened. The daddy-to-be stepped inside. Following close on his heels were the other two people who had been in the room when she woke.

Sean shouldered his way past Jake and the hussy in gold. "Sis," he said, sitting on the bed beside her. A small smile softened the worry on his face. "The doc says you're okay."

"I'm fine. Just a little tired. I guess that's normal." She ducked her head to avoid his gaze.

"It's true? You're pregnant?"

"It's not official but, yeah, I think I might be." She raised her head, seeking Jake's gaze. The crinkles around his blue eyes matched the parenthesis around his curved lips.

"It's mine."

She nodded. "Yes. No other possibilities." No use denying it. He, of all people, knew she wouldn't have gone to anyone else when he left. It was a shame she couldn't say the same about him. As much as she tried not to, she glanced at the woman standing across the room. Why was she still here?

"Oh." Jake beckoned his date forward. "You remember Kelly. You met her downstairs."

Sean stood, making way for them to approach the bed. Humiliation threatened to take away her newly discovered joy, but she lifted her chin, determined to see this meeting through with a measure of dignity, if possible. As much as she hated Jake at that moment, she had to think of her child. She wanted her kid to have a relationship with its father. If that meant playing nice with this or whatever woman he was fucking at the time, then she would do it.

"Siobhan," Kelly said, taking the place Sean had vacated. "I can't tell you how excited I am to meet you. Daddy told me all about you. He went on and on until I couldn't stand it another minute. I told him to get his ass back to Texas and do whatever it took to get you back." She literally bounced with enthusiasm. Her eyes mirrored her smile, both looking eerily familiar. "I can't believe I'm going to have a brother or a sister! That is so cool." The young woman glanced up at Jake, whose face had paled. "Way to go, Dad. Who'd a thought you had it in you?"

"Wait." Siobhan held her hand up. "What's going on here?" Her gaze darted between the two people closest to her. "Jake, who is this woman?"

His face turned bright red. She'd never seen him look more like a kid caught with his hand in the cookie jar. "I knew this was a bad idea, but Kelly talked me into it."

"Hey!" Gold lame girl squealed. "You didn't have to go along with it."

"Talked you into what?"

Jake glared at Kelly before turning his attention to Siobhan. He shook his head. "I'm sorry, babe. Like I said, it was a bad idea, but I was desperate to catch your attention, so I went along with it. Kelly isn't my date. She's my daughter."

Bees buzzed inside her skull. Surely, she'd misunderstood. "Your *what?*"

"My daughter. My twenty-year-old daughter."

"Twenty." Five years younger than her. "Oh, boy."

"Siobhan." Kelly patted her leg to get her attention. She looked into eyes so familiar they made her heart ache. "I'm so sorry. If I'd had any idea…well, I never would have suggested Dad try to make you jealous. It was a stupid thing to do."

Had she ever been that young, that clueless? *You still are. That young. Maybe not so clueless anymore.*

"This isn't your fault. Jake should have known better." She glared at the man in question. He was too old to be playing childish games with people's feelings. He had the good sense to appear contrite, at least.

"I'm going to get out of here, let you two be alone, but I want you to know how happy I am to meet you. Dad was miserable without you. He's never been that way about a woman before, so I knew you had to be special. I can see you're everything he said you were."

"Thanks," she said, meaning it. It wasn't the girl's fault her dad was an ass. She accepted Kelly's congratulations on her presumed pregnancy then watched as the girl left, taking her whirlwind enthusiasm with her.

"I'll see you tomorrow," her brother vowed.

She was certain he had more in mind than a casual sibling meet-up. *Big brother lecture number two million coming right up.* Sean followed the younger woman out, promising to see her safely home.

She was alone with Jake.

"So." Jake shuffled his feet, wanting to jump in the bed with her, hold her close, marvel at the wonder of his child growing inside he. Not wanting to end up on his ass if she didn't want him there, he stayed where he was.

"You have a daughter?"

He nodded. Looking at the floor was so much safer than seeing the pain he'd etched onto her face. "Yeah."

"You didn't think this was something I should know?"

He shook his head. "I was afraid you

would think I was some kind of pervert. You know, looking for a twisted, incestuous fuck. It wasn't like that with you. It never was." He shifted, turned his gaze on her, willing his next words to make a difference. "You're light years older than Kelly in every way that counts."

"She's not a child, Jake."

He scrubbed a hand over his face. "Don't I know it." He took that first step toward her, stopping short. "She makes me feel old, but when I'm with you, I feel like a teenager again. I love you. I love you so much it scares the shit out of me." She hadn't tried to run from him yet, so he took another step closer to the bed.

"I don't know how you ended up pregnant." He grinned. "Well, I do know, but we were careful. I was careful. Just in case you think this is an apology, it's not. I'm not the least bit sorry you're pregnant." He hoped he'd put the right amount of inflection in that last statement, hoped she would hear it as an invitation to tell him how she felt about the child.

"I was there, Jake. I know you were

careful. If I'm pregnant, it was an accident. I get that."

"Do you think you're pregnant?"

"Yes, I do. All the signs are there. I've been ignoring them for weeks, dismissing them as dep—"

"Depression?" He closed the distance between them, dropping to his knees beside the bed. Taking her hand in his, he brushed his thumbs over her translucent skin. "I'm so sorry, babe. I never should have left you."

"I know what you said when you left. Would you care to tell me the truth now?"

He nodded, looking down at her hand in his. "I was nineteen when Amy got pregnant with Kelly. Heading off to my first Minor League assignment. Even if that lifestyle had been a good one for a family, which it wasn't, not by a long stretch, Amy and I weren't in love. She didn't want to spend her life with me. I didn't even try to convince her to. I had no idea if I would ever be able to provide a stable home or make a living for us, so I left. I sent her money, made legal arrangements for Kelly's care. Amy never tried to keep me from seeing her. I spent as much time as I could with her. I have a home near her in Denver."

"That's where you disappear to in the off season?"

"Yeah. Amy wanted Kel to have a normal upbringing, so I've done my best to keep her out of the media spotlight. Her last name is Porter. Amy's name."

"I don't see you agreeing to that."

He'd shrugged off the long-ago hurt. "I didn't like the idea, but at the time, it was the right thing to do. Less questions Amy would have to answer about the father of her child. Less confusion for Kel at school. That sort of thing."

Head bowed, he nearly fell over when she stroked his hair with her free hand. *She* was offering *him* comfort. If he hadn't already been on his knees, he would have fallen. Only his Siobhan would show that kind of compassion to a man who'd knocked her up then left town.

"She looks like you. She has your eyes, your smile."

"You think so?" He dared to look up at the woman he loved. Her skin had lost the pallor acquired when she fainted. Her cheeks were rosy. Her skin glowed as it had every time he'd seen her the last few weeks.

"I do. She's beautiful, just like her father."

He was stunned by her admission. "You think I'm beautiful?"

"Handsome, sexy on the outside, beautiful on the inside. You did what was best for your daughter at the expense of what you wanted."

"You make me sound like a saint," he protested. "I did what was right at the time. I've protected her privacy for a long time—it's just something I do without thinking. She'll always be my little girl, I guess. I should have told you about her weeks ago."

"Would it have changed anything if you had?"

"I honestly don't know." He held her hand prisoner, afraid if he let go, she'd bolt. "I've made a lot of mistakes in my life, but you and this baby aren't on that list. Since we're being honest here, Kel was the excuse, but I ran because I was afraid you'd wake up one day, see an old man in your bed. That would be the end of me."

"You left because you didn't trust my love for you." She pulled her hand from his grasp. "I need to go home."

He balled his hand into a fist in an effort to preserve her touch. "I'll take you home."

"No. I'll catch a cab downstairs."

The tiny sliver of hope he'd been holding onto evaporated into the icy air between them. He'd fucked up to the point she didn't even want to accept a ride from him. Unable to think of a single argument to change her mind, he let her walk out of his life.

CHAPTER THIRTEEN

Present - Christmas Eve

"I think you've lost your mind."

Siobhan was glad her back was to her brother, so he couldn't see her rolling her eyes. He sounded like a broken record. She grabbed two water bottles from the fridge then joined him in the small living room.

"Are you going to tell me that every day until you die?" *Wasn't two weeks enough?*

"Maybe," he said, not an ounce of remorse in his voice. "I don't understand why you won't talk to Jake. He's got as much at stake in this as you do."

She propped her feet on the edge of the coffee table. "He's the sperm donor. Nothing more."

"Do you hear yourself? That's the bitchiest thing I've ever heard you say."

She acknowledged the truth of his statement by raising her plastic bottle in salute. "Yes, I suppose it is. But it's the truth."

"No, it's not. If that's all he was, he wouldn't offer to marry you. He loves you."

She shook her head. "He feels guilty, that's all. The he-man used protection. It failed. He's going to do the right thing, sacrifice his freedom on the altar of marriage."

"I don't think he sees it that way."

"That's the way I see it. In case you don't know, my opinion is the only one that counts." If he really wanted to marry her, he would have asked when he first returned to Dallas. His lame proposal the day she'd come back from the doctor with a positive pregnancy test proved one thing—he would sacrifice his happiness for his child, just as he'd done when he gave in to Amy's mother instead of insisting Kelly have his last name.

"Yeah, I get that it's your body, yadda, yadda, yadda. But half of the kid you're carrying is Jake's. You can cut him out of your life, but you can't cut him out of his child's life."

"I know that. That's one of the reasons I let my lease go on my condo in D.C. I'm uprooting my entire life, so he can see his kid."

"Is that the only reason?"

The soft way he posed the question indicated he suspected her of fraud where Jake was concerned. He was right. She didn't want Jake to marry her just because she was pregnant, but she couldn't bring herself to go back to D.C. either.

"Siobhan? Talk to me."

"What do you want me to say, that I love him?" She blinked at the ceiling, willing the moisture gathering in her eyes to go away. "Okay. I love him. Are you happy now?"

"No. I won't be happy until you're

happy. You aren't going to be happy until you forgive Jake for leaving. He came back, sis. *Before* he knew you were pregnant. Hell, he came back before you knew you were pregnant. I find it hard to believe you're holding out because of that. So, are you going to tell me what's really going on inside that hard head of yours?"

No.

He shifted on the sofa, leaning forward to rest his elbows on his knees. "Okay, so here's what I think. His age didn't mean much to you until you found out you're barely older than his daughter. A few months ago, you were pissed at me for pointing out that it was a possibility. My guess is, you're feeling…used? Freaked?"

She squirmed beneath his steady gaze, not to mention his spot-on assessment of her state of mind. "So, you were right. He has a kid my age. I was wrong."

"I was wrong, sis. *I* was wrong." He poked a finger at his chest. "Not you. I judged the guy without knowing all the facts. Back then, he did what was right for all of them—Kelly, her mother…him. He didn't love Kelly's mother. But he loves you. He wants to marry you. He came here to propose—*before* he knew about the kid. Yeah, he was an ass for leaving in the first place, but I'm a guy, I can tell you, we do stupid things sometimes. But he came to his senses. He realized the age thing didn't mean as much as he thought it did."

Sean sat back though his gaze remained fixed on her, no doubt waiting for her to admit he was right.

"At least give the guy a chance. Aren't you the person who writes sappy love stories about people overcoming impossible odds to be together?"

She was, once. "It's called fiction for a reason. It isn't real."

"So says the woman who is afraid to write her own happily-ever-after ending." He stood, ruffling her hair like she was still a kid. "Prince Charming is waiting for your call."

"He always has to have the last word," she mumbled to herself as her brother traversed the walkway to the main house. "Prince Charming. There's no such thing."

For the first time in months, she opened her laptop with the intention of writing something productive. The blank white screen representation of a piece of paper stared back at her. If she could write her own happy ever after, what would it be?

It's fiction. You can write any impossible thing you want.

She placed her fingers on the keys.

Once upon a time....

A knock on the door startled her. She mistyped the word climax as climacx, hastily backspaced to fix it, saved the work in progress, then went to the door. She flipped the light switches, illuminating the room and the porch. The day had somehow morphed into evening without her noticing. She hadn't gotten that lost in her writing since before she'd met Jake.

Expecting to find her brother on the other side of the door, she swung it open. The harsh words intended to end his daily interference in her life died on her lips. *Not Sean.*

"Jake."

"Siobhan."

Her fingers tightened on the doorknob. Damn him for looking like the hero in every fantasy she'd ever had, including the one she'd been writing all afternoon.

"Your brother mentioned you didn't have a Christmas tree."

She followed his gaze to the scraggly evergreen beside him.

"Last one on the lot." He gave it a little shake. Tiny greenish-brown spikes showered the doorstep.

On the verge of protesting the mess, she glanced at her visitor. The plea written in the lines of his face stopped her.

"I didn't want to be alone tonight."

If he'd brought anything else, said anything else, she would have slammed the door in his face, but how could she turn him away when he looked more forlorn than the stubby tree dangling from his gloved fist. She stepped back, issuing a silent invitation for him to enter.

She closed the door behind him. He stood the emaciated plant on the floor. It leaned precariously to one side on a makeshift stand nailed to the bottom.

Jake proceeded to remove his coat and gloves, tossing them over the nearest chair. He smelled like pine mixed with winter cold right before it snowed. The tips of his ears and nose were red. Bright spots of color dotted his cheeks. He turned, focused his gaze on her. The warmth in his gaze melted some of the ice around her heart.

You've been reading your own writing again. Stop it. He's not your Prince Charming or a hero. He has his own agenda. Remember that.

"I think it might snow." He blew into his cupped hands. "It sure feels like it could. Wouldn't that be something, a white Christmas in Dallas?"

She hadn't given it much thought, but she supposed a blanket of white would be an anomaly for the area. "I guess."

Undeterred by her short answer, her visitor set about finding a place for his less than majestic gift. After trying a few options, he settled on the coffee table as the perfect spot to display the orphaned conifer. Curled up at one end of the sofa, she watched him fuss with it as if it was a stately specimen instead of a reject from a mass deforestation project.

"There." He sat to admire his work. "Perfect."

Siobhan snickered. "If you say so."

"What?" He feigned being stabbed in the heart. "This tree spoke to me on the lot. I had to give it a home."

"What did it say? 'Hey, sucker, over here?'"

His expression grew serious. "No. It said, 'I need someone to love me, just like you do.'"

"Jake…."

Coming around the table, he lowered himself to the opposite end of the sofa as if he expected the cushion to explode the moment he touched down. "Please, Siobhan, give me another chance. One night. That's all I'm asking. Let me stay with you tonight. Let me hold you in my arms again. Waking up next to you on Christmas morning would be the best gift I can imagine."

"What about your daughter?"

"Kelly went home to Colorado. I promised I'd go back next week to see her and my parents."

She turned her face away,

remembering how her parents had reacted when she'd finally called to tell them of her pregnancy. In one short phone call, she went from being their favorite child, the one who could do no wrong, to an outcast. How had Sean stood it all these years? She'd always admired her brother for his strength but, until she stood in his shoes, she'd no idea how difficult being disowned had been on him.

"Sean told me what your parents did. I'm so sorry. That's my fault, too."

"No." She shook her head. "I wanted you from the first moment I saw you. I practically begged you."

"That's bullshit. I took advantage. God, the minute you stepped out of that car and opened your mouth...I lost it. I was a goner. I couldn't wait to get you in my bed, to claim you."

She swiped moisture from her eyes. "I'm sorry," she sniffled. "I'm usually not a crier."

"It's the hormones," he said, sounding like an authority on the subject.

She cocked her head to one side in question.

He shrugged. "That's what all the blogs say."

"You read pregnancy blogs?"

He sighed, relaxing since nothing had exploded. "I'm serious, Siobhan. Even if you won't have me, I'm going to be a part of my child's life. I missed everything with Kelly. This time is going to be different."

A giant ball of emotion formed in her chest, threatening to choke her.

"I didn't return because of the baby. I came back for you." He stretched his hand out to her, palm up. "I love you. I want you to be my wife."

Jake trembled while the only woman he'd ever loved stared at his outstretched hand as if it held a cobra ready to strike instead of his heart. Tears spilled undeterred down her flushed cheeks, each one like acid eating away at his confidence. He couldn't bear to see her upset. Knowing he'd brought her to this state cut him to the core.

What could he do? Withdrawing his hand, he stood. He'd call Sean, tell him to come check on her. "I'll go."

She looked so fragile sitting there curled into a ball, it was all he could do not to scoop her into his arms. He longed to tell her everything would be all right. She wasn't a child. She was a full-grown woman capable of making decisions about her life. Her decision regarding him was painfully clear.

As he drew closer, her eyelids dropped. Reaching out, he cupped her damp cheek in his palm. Tilting her face up, he leaned in to place a soft kiss on her trembling lips. She didn't respond, not even to protest. Drinking in her scent for the last time, he committed the moment to memory. The last time he would touch her.

Drawing a small box from his pocket, he placed it under the tree. Maybe she'd sell it or perhaps keep it for their child. Whatever. He'd purchased the ring for her, so she should have it. "Merry Christmas."

CHAPTER FOURTEEN

Present - Christmas Eve

Jake paused on the sidewalk. Siobhan's brother was celebrating inside the main house with Bentley and Ashley. He suspected their association was anything but traditional, but it was their business, not his. Besides, who was he to judge? He'd only had one serious relationship in his entire life, and look how he'd fucked that up. Whatever the three of them had going, he wished them all the best.

For reasons of personal safety, he decided against a face-to-face with Sean. Stopping, he pulled out his cell phone. He was scrolling through his contacts list when a triangle of light swept across the walk.

"Jake."

He turned. Siobhan stood in the open doorway, one hand braced against the frame. Her feet were bare, the toes of one curled, resting atop the other. Hope flared bright, but he squished it down before it could take over. She probably just wanted to return his gift.

"You should go back inside. It's cold." *That's the best you can do? What an asshole.*

"I know." She wrapped her arms around her middle. The luscious body he longed to hold trembled from head to toe.

It was all he could do to stay where he was, let her say what she needed to say, when every cell in his body wanted to protect her. But the only thing she needed protection from was him.

"You shouldn't be alone tonight." Her words were fuel to the spark of hope he'd tried to extinguish moments before.

With the light behind her and only the weak glow of the porch light to illuminate her face, he could barely make out her features. What was she saying, exactly? He took a cautious step closer.

"I don't want to be alone, not ever again.".

The hand she stretched out to him shone pale in the dark night. "Come inside."

Shutting the door, he leaned against it, not sure why he'd been invited back inside. Siobhan resumed her seat on the sofa, her knees brought up to her chin, her arms securing them. Her cheeks and nose were rosy from the cold, her eyes red from crying.

"I was just going to call Sean, let him know you were alone so he could check on you later."

She nodded. "I appreciate your concern, but I'm not planning on being alone."

He raised his brows. "Oh?" Hope rekindled, but he wasn't ready to put words in her mouth yet.

"I was planning on sleeping with my fiancé tonight."

He'd never believed in spontaneous human combustion until that moment. Fortunately, he was several feet from the sorry excuse for a tree he'd brought her or it would be in danger of going up in flames.

"What changed your mind?" He held up his hand. "Wait. You're talking about me, right? You aren't engaged to someone else, are you?"

"I'm talking about you. No one else. Never anyone else."

He didn't dare get closer, not until he understood her abrupt about-face. "A few minutes ago, you wanted me to leave and never come back."

"I thought you were proposing to me because of the baby. I wanted you to marry me because you love me, not because I'm pregnant."

"Wasn't that what I said? I could have sworn I said I love you somewhere in there."

"You did," she acknowledged. "But I needed to be sure."

He stared at her. "I'm confused. For just a second, could you bring this down to the level of us poor, clueless males of the species? 'Cause I don't know what the fuck you're talking about."

She smiled, uncurling from the sofa. Picking up the small velvet ring box, she opened the lid. "This jewelry store is in Denver."

"Yeah." *What the fuck does that have to do with anything?*

"You bought the ring *before* you came back to Dallas. Before you knew about the baby."

Stars shone and angels sang. It was a Christmas miracle. He smiled. "I did."

"So, you didn't ask me to marry you because of the baby."

"No, I didn't."

"Ask me again. Please?"

He lifted his face to the ceiling, mouthed the words, "Thank you, God." Pushing off the door, he crossed to her, dropping to one knee in front of her. She placed the open ring box in his hand. Head bowed, he clutched it tight. The words were there, he'd actually said them earlier, but that had been when he was virtually certain she would turn him down. She was giving him a do-over, and he wanted to get it right this time, because this time, she might say yes.

"Give me a second. I've made a mess of everything so far. I don't want to add this to the list."

"Take your time. But if you don't come up with something in the next thirty seconds, I'm going to take matters into my own hands."

She would. That's one of the things he loved about her, she didn't wait for things to happen to her. She made them happen. Like the night they met.

He looked up at her. She gazed back at him with all the shattered innocence of a fallen angel. His fallen angel. God, he loved her. He'd waited longer than most to find the woman who made him want to be a better man, and stupid fuck that he was, he'd almost let her get away.

"The night we met, you dazzled me. I'd never wanted a woman the way I wanted you. But it was more than a physical reaction, though that was pretty hard to ignore. You were so damned sure of yourself, of what you wanted. That night…." The memory nearly strangled him. He cleared his throat before continuing. "I'd never felt anything as wonderful as you. Nothing. I don't know how to explain it but to say it wasn't just physical. I know. The words are inadequate, but I know you felt it, too. I saw it in your eyes. I think you saw it in mine. I shut you out after that. I can't tell you how sorry I am for doing that to you. I'd spent my life running from commitment, and there it was, there you were. Commitment was written on the wall above the bed in neon block letters.

"Anyway, you know I couldn't stay away from you after that. I kept telling myself you were no different than all the others. When the time came, I would walk away from you just like always. Only you *were* different. Before my plane landed in Colorado, I knew I'd made a huge mistake. I was happy to see Kelly, but I was miserable inside. I'd left my heart here, in your hands."

He took her hands in his. "On my daughter's advice, I bought a ring, hatched that stupid plan with Ashley, and came back to grovel at your feet. Turns out, I'm lousy at groveling. You wouldn't give me the time of day."

He shifted. This is where he needed to get it right. Most guys got one chance, this was his third...his last. *Three strikes—you're out.* "Now that I have your undivided attention...Siobhan Flannery, I love you more than I ever thought possible. I've used every excuse in the book to push you out of my heart, but you're still there. You always will be. I can't imagine my future without you in it. I want to hold you in my arms every night and see your smile first thing every morning for the rest of my days. You own my heart and my soul. I love you. Will you make me the happiest man on the planet? Will you marry me?"

Lord, she was going to cry. Again. He held his breath, waiting for her to say something. He'd just bared his soul to her, and his bum knee was cramping. If she didn't answer soon, he was going to have to call someone to help him get off the floor.

"Siobhan?" he prodded.

Her head bobbed. A tear streaked her cheek. "Yes," she whispered. Then stronger. "Yes."

His hands shook so much he thought he might drop the ring before he got it on her finger. But being a woman who made things happen, Siobhan helped him slide the glittering band past her knuckles.

She was his. *Thank God.*

Siobhan almost laughed at the play of emotions crossing Jake's face. Panic when she took her time answering. Relief when she finally got the single syllable past her lips. Panic again when he realized what he'd done. He'd made a game out of avoiding commitment, so proposing hadn't come easy for him.

Reining in the guffaws she knew he wouldn't appreciate, she smiled instead. Reaching out, she cupped his face between her palms. His eyes were glazed, his lips trembling. The idea of committing to one person for the rest of her life scared her, too. But there was one thing she knew would banish their nerves. It was something they'd always done well together. Leaning forward so her lips almost brushed his, she whispered, "Make love to me."

There it was—the spark of desire that had shown bright even in the darkened parking lot the night they'd met. It still had the same effect on her— instant meltdown.

"Your wish is my command." He canted his head to one side, taking her mouth with a kiss that belied his statement. Jake took command, as she'd known he would, taking what he wanted with such tender demands she gave willingly. His hands claimed her body with fevered precision, mapping her curves like an explorer searching for a long lost trail. Each touch was familiar, yet different—deeper, if that was possible.

She was breathless when he broke the kiss in order to scoop her up in his arms. Setting her on her feet beside the bed, he made short work of removing her clothes.

"I want to see you." He stepped back to admire her as if she were a museum piece. His eyes gleamed as his gaze swept over her. "You're so damned beautiful." His voice was reverent as he reached out to trace the swell of her breasts. She stood still, while his hands traveled paths he'd known well before he left. "Your tits are bigger."

She nodded. "Tender, too." Aching for his touch. She drew her shoulders back, thrusting the heavy orbs toward him. But his gaze had traveled lower, to her stomach. She sucked in a breath when his fingers fluttered over the still flat plane. "Our baby is in there."

He lifted his head. His eyes were filled with wonder—a feeling she was becoming intimate with. A new life grew inside her. Jake's baby. *Their* baby.

"It's a miracle. You're a miracle." His hand flattened on her stomach, the other on the small of her back, drawing her to him. "I didn't know what it was like to love until I saw you, then *wham*, I was done for."

His hand stroked her belly, going lower with each circular pass until his fingers brushed her swollen mons. Her nipples were hard peaks against the knobby wool of his sweater. She rubbed herself back and forth, whimpering at the painfully erotic sensations shooting from the throbbing peaks to her pussy.

"Shh, sweetheart," he crooned against her neck. His lips, teeth, and tongue assaulted the tender skin at her neck.

Lower.

"I'm going to take care of you, tonight and always."

"Please," she begged, opening her legs wider to allow his fingers better access. She couldn't get close enough to him. She needed him inside her, needed his weight pressing against her, needed all of him.

She nearly crumpled when he stepped away, but he caught her with one arm while he pulled the bedclothes back with the other. The sheets felt like ice against her back, but watching Jake remove his clothes ignited a roaring blaze inside her. His body was a work of art— all hard planes and angles honed from years of workouts. A man's body.

His maturity had intrigued her from the beginning. *My very own seasoned veteran.*

Her mouth watered when his cock sprang free of his briefs. Her thighs fell open—inviting, anticipating.

The cocky smile on his face said he knew exactly what to do with her offering. Climbing onto the bed, he stretched out beside her. Using one elbow to prop himself up, he placed one big, heated palm on her stomach. The heavy weight of his erection rested against her hip. She reached for it, only to be stopped by his strong fingers clasped around her wrist.

"In a minute, babe." His gaze skimmed her from neck to toes then back up, stopping where his hand claimed her. "I've missed you, missed your body. I want to take my time."

"It's been so long." She stroked his chest to make her meaning clear.

"No one knows that more than me, sweetheart. Be a good girl, put your hands behind your head." She did as she was told, willing to play his games for a few minutes.

His fingertips skimming up her torso made her groan. "Patience, little one. I won't leave you unsatisfied. I promise."

He bent, placed a chaste kiss on one distended nipple. "Some of the few benefits of getting older—for a man—are stamina and patience." His next kiss to her nipple could only be described as leisurely. In no hurry at all, he made love to her breast, teasing with his tongue, grazing the tight nub with his teeth until she was a whimpering mass of need. She arched her back, begging for more. *Patience be damned.*

The dark scruff of his beard abraded the tip as he looked up at her. "Don't move unless I tell you to."

She raised her head, her gaze locking with his. The banked flames there sent a surge of power through her. She would follow his orders, but she was the one in control. His delay tactics were as much for his enjoyment as they were for hers.

Letting her head drop back to her folded hands, she answered with a contented sigh.

It seemed like an eternity, during which Jake explored every inch of her body, kissing, tasting, claiming, before he finally spread her thighs wide and drove deep inside her.

No protection. Skin to skin.

She tilted her hips to take more of him.

"Christ, Siobhan," he hissed. His cock pulsed inside her.

"Jake," she breathed, not daring to move again. "You make me feel…whole."

Propped on his forearms, his hands bracketing her face, he rained kisses on her eyelids, her cheeks, the corners of her lips. "I want to stay this way forever." He shifted his hips just enough to heighten the sensation.

"I'm good with that," she said, stroking his back from shoulders to his firm ass. Images of him carrying her around all day, his cock buried in her pussy, her legs locked around his hips formed in her mind. She giggled.

"What's so funny?" he asked, smiling down at her.

She described the picture in her head. "It's funny, but I'd do it if I could. I don't want to be apart from you ever again, Jake. Not for a minute."

He flexed his hips, pulling almost all the way out, slowly filling her again. "You won't be. I'm going to keep you pregnant, so you'll always have a part of me inside you. I can't wait to see you big and round with my baby."

"Jake." Her voice was nothing more than a whispered emotion.

"We need a code word, like a safe word. Only when you say it, I'll know you want me to make love to you."

"Seasoned veteran."

He smiled. "Sounds like one of your book titles."

As if he'd turned the key to her imagination, words, scenes, and characters flew through her mind. "Only if you're my hero."

"I never want to be anything else, babe. Just say the word. I'm at your service. Twenty-four/seven. Anywhere. Anytime."

She looped her fingers at his nape, pulled his face down to hers. Her gaze took in the lines so dear to her, the hint of gray peppering his temples, his lips, wet and waiting. Just before their mouths touched, she said the words. "Seasoned veteran."

ABOUT THE AUTHOR

USA Today Bestselling Author, Roz Lee is a displaced Texan who lives in New Jersey with her husband of almost four decades, and Bud, an overly large rescue dog who demands regular romps in the woods no matter how busy his parents are.

The mom of two daughters, one a police officer and the other an economist married to a pilot, Roz collects Depression glass, and teacups with rose patterns. Her favorite food is Tex-Mex, and she's never met a piece of chocolate she didn't like.

When Roz isn't writing, she's reading, or traipsing around the country on one adventure or another. Warning—she brakes for antique stores!

Made in United States
North Haven, CT
12 September 2024

57304919R00089